The Royal Diaries

Sŏndŏk

Princess of the Moon and Stars

BY SHERI HOLMAN

Scholastic Inc. New York

Korea
A.D. 595

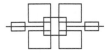

15th day of the 11th moon, +
16th year of King Chinp'yŏng
Tŏngji (Winter solstice),
Half-moon Fortress, Kŭmsŏng, Silla

Happy Little New Year, Grandmother!

We wear our red silk *chima* and eat red bean porridge to keep the evil spirits away on this, the shortest day of the year. My sisters Sŏnwha, Ch'ŏn-myong, and I, along with all the ladies at court, have dyed our fingernails a deep crimson with balsam. Ghosts are such cowards about the color red! Tonight is the one night of the year I will not brave the long, lonely darkness to make my star calculations. I do not want evil spirits tangling in my hair.

I am writing, Grandmother, because Mother has given me responsibility for you, our Ancestor Jar. As a little girl, I remember staring up at you — a beautiful pale green jar, brimming with white rice and paper. Mother explained that this jar was the symbol of all our long-dead Kim ancestors, and that we must bow to it as we would to our own flesh and blood. I longed to write prayers and place them inside you, making offerings as a grown-up lady would. Now, every day I shall write a message to you. I will fill you with prayers and hymns and offer you fresh bowls of water and rice cakes at all the proper festivals. In return, I hope you will bless our family with good fortune and keep all evil influences away.

Starting tonight.

Later

I have been thinking over my duties as keeper of the Ancestor Jar, and I hope you will not grow angry with me if I slip in some of my own private thoughts. I know this is not customary, but as I get older and inherit more responsibilities, I am finding myself in need of guidance, Grandmother. You were wise and just in your life. If I cannot be a son to my father, I hope you will help me to become his most dutiful daughter. If you ever become unhappy with this arrangement, I hope you will let me know.

Later still

Forgive me for being so talkative, Grandmother, I know you are trying to sleep. I am just so excited. Word has reached me that the ambassador from China has arrived with the new official calendar. I've heard he is a great lover of astronomy and I hope to learn much from him during his stay.

16th day of the 11th moon, 16th year of King Chinp'yŏng

They say in China there grows a flower called *ming chia*. It is a miraculous calendar flower that gains one petal each day for fifteen days until the full moon and then loses one petal a day until the dark of the moon. When I was a child, I always imagined the Chinese astronomers with potted flowers on their writing tables, carefully noting the birth or fall of each petal. Now I know the difficult calculations they must make to chart the movements of the sun and moon. Because our calendar is based on the phases of the moon, as well as the sun, it needs constant adjustment. Not only must the new year be calculated afresh, but the astronomers must determine certain "leap" months every few years. A proper calendar must also account for solar and lunar eclipses.

This is what I love most about studying astronomy, Grandmother. It is not just a science of planets and stars. It is a science about their marvelously complex relationships to one another. Just think, Grandmother — there are two forces perpetually at work in the universe: the *um* principle (that which our Chinese neighbors would call *ying*) that represents all that is dark, negative, and feminine in the world; and the *yang* principle, representing the light, positive, and masculine forces. For the universe to function, *um* and *yang* must stay in perfect balance. There can be no positive force without a negative force — just as there can be no day without night.

I caught only a glimpse of the Chinese ambassador today, when he was crossing the courtyard with Father. He was tall and grave looking, dressed in long black robes like a scholar and wearing the high, peaked hat of the Confucians. He appears to be very learned, Grandmother, and I greatly desire to make his acquaintance.

17th day of the 11th moon,
16th day of King Chinp'yŏng

I sat up late last night, writing down questions to ask the ambassador about his country's methods for measuring the stars. This morning, I decided I could wait no longer and walked out to see if I might "accidentally" encounter him. I walked past the administrative buildings and past the Grand Hall. I even went looking for him down near the lake where he had been spotted, but sadly he was no longer there. I did have a nice surprise, however. My old friend Chajang was home for a visit.

I spied him on the other side of the lake where he stopped to watch the servants cut ice for the Royal Ice House. The men cut deep blocks from the frozen lake, then drag them by rope to the artificial cave where they will be covered with straw to preserve them through the summer. While I cannot imagine it now, one day I suppose it will be warm again.

I had seen very little of my old friend since he has joined the *hwarang,* Father's Flower Princes. Not only do these young Flower Princes work to defend our kingdom, Silla, from her enemies, they also write beautiful poems and pay court to ladies. Father calls them the pride of the kingdom. They are the best and bravest boys from all the aristocratic families. They do Silla credit in battle and will soon be off to fight against our enemy, Paekche.

"Little Herdboy!" I cried, using my old nickname for him. "What are you doing back at the Fortress?"

"Weaving Maid!" he called back when he saw me. When I was first learning the names of the stars, I was enchanted by the romantic story of the Herdboy and Weaving Maid who fell in love but could meet only once a year. When we were children Chajang and I fancied ourselves in love and called each other by those names. But that was childish silliness, so long ago.

"There is little we can do outside in this weather," he said, coming around to my side of the lake. "Since we cannot drill, we are using the winter to study poetry and the ways of the Buddha. While I love the arts of war, I must confess peace suits me better."

In my mind's eye, Grandmother, Chajang is still a boy, spinning tops on the frozen ground. But somewhere along the way he seems to have become a man. Though at thirteen, he is only one year younger than I am, he is a full head taller. He wears his hair in a topknot and his ears are bright with golden earrings.

"You look well, Lady Sŏndŏk," he said, for we are older now and must be more formal with each other.

"As do you."

I told him I was searching for the ambassador from China who had brought along the new calendar. Chajang thought it funny I should still be stargazing, when my father had always disapproved. He assumed I had moved on to more womanly tasks.

"Father will eventually come around," I said. "The

stars reflect the royal family. What better person to interpret them than a member of it?"

He walked me back to the Princesses' Hall where we said our good-byes. It was several hours later before I realized I had completely forgotten my search for the ambassador!

19th day of the 11th moon,
16th year of King Chinp'yŏng
Late in the Hour of the Dog

I hope you are not too cold, Grandmother. I am padded in my quilted robes and wrapped in furs, but your ceramic sides are exposed to the frigid night air.

I have brought you outside to see my favorite stargazing spot, a rocky plateau inside Half-moon Fortress with an unobstructed view of the heavens. It is my greatest desire to one day build an observatory here dedicated only to mapping the sky. I have hinted to Father that is what I want for my New Year's gift. Please, Grandmother, if you have any influence on your son, use it to secure me my own observatory.

What I told Chajang is true: as the stars govern the

workings of the royal family, and as our actions affect the stars, who better to read them than a royal princess? It is a ruler's great responsibility to control the heavens and the weather and all natural phenomena. If we are careless and anger the gods, they will punish our people by bringing hail or great lightning to ruin the crops. But if we are good and follow the will of Heaven, then all will prosper in our kingdom. My sisters give no thought to this responsibility. Ch'ŏn-myong is dutiful and good, helping Mother sew and tend the kitchen. She keeps her eyes perpetually lowered over her work. Sŏnwha has eyes for nothing other than the mirror. Her gaze is fixed on her own lovely face and silken hair, and her thoughts are only of her future husband, whomever he might be. But I am heir to the throne, and I must give my mind over to weightier matters. It is my fondest hope that the Chinese ambassador will have word of new theories and technologies that might help me better understand the sky I am to rule one day. Though Silla is advanced, we can always learn more from our neighbor to the north.

Let me take a few measurements, Grandmother, and then I will get you back inside where it is warm.

20th day of the 11th moon,
16th year of King Chinp'yŏng

Father has sent word that I may meet Lord Lin Fang (as I have learned the ambassador is called) when our court astronomers present our calendar tomorrow. Father does not know how closely I worked with our scientists on charting the moon and stars, for I swore them to secrecy. Father does not wholly approve of my love of this science, though I hope to convince him it is an asset.

While the new calendar is very important, a courier could have brought it as easily as an ambassador, which leads me to believe Father seeks a closer alliance with the Sui Emperor of China. Silla desires access to the Yellow Sea and our enemy Paekche blocks us. Over the years, there have been many shifting alliances between the three kingdoms of ancient Chŏsŏn. Remember, Grandmother, when Koguryŏ was once the most powerful of the three kingdoms? Then it owned land deep into the Cold North Plain. But the Chinese grew afraid of our neighbor to the north and began attacking where they could. At one time we were allied with Paekche against Koguryŏ, but now those two states ally themselves against us, and we must look to our powerful neighbor, China, if we are to survive.

I know this is why Father gives special deference to Lord Lin Fang. If China joined our enemies, we would be wiped from the earth.

21st day of the 11th moon, 16th year of King Chinp'yŏng

Today is the day. At last I meet the ambassador. I will write of the event in detail later, Grandmother. Now I must dress and be off.

Later

By the time I arrived and left my shoes outside on the porch, the hall was filled with court officials and members of the aristocratic True Bone families in their varying ranks. The presenting of the calendar is always a very crowded event, for the landowners must pass the information along to the farmers so that they will know when to plant their crops and hold their festivals. I saw my friend Chajang in the crowd and nodded a brief hello.

I took my place beside Father as the only other member of the Holy Bone royal family. To my delight, the ambassador stood on his other side as Father's honored guest.

Lord Lin Fang is even more imposing up close than at a distance, Grandmother. He has a thin gray beard and eyebrows so overgrown they curl like tiger's whiskers. His gaze is knowing and serious and he seems to hold a million secrets. Father presented me and I bowed deeply.

Lord Lin Fang seemed surprised to see me, a girl, at such an important gathering, and even more startled to learn I was my father's heir.

"I know it is unusual, Lord Fang," said Father, explaining. "But here in Silla, only those born of the Holy Bone rank might inherit the throne. This rank is limited to myself, my brothers, my children, and my sons-in-law. Sadly, my two brothers are dead, and Queen Ma-ya has bore me no son. Thus Sŏndŏk is my heir apparent."

Lin Fang gave me a small, polite nod then turned his attention to the assembly.

After our astronomers (with much pomp and formality) presented our calendar, the ambassador rose to deliver greetings from the Chinese emperor. For nearly an hour we heard about his Celestial Majesty, the Son of Heaven in China. We heard about his virtues and piety and accomplishments. About what a patron of the arts he was, and how brave in war. About how the heavens stopped and listened to all that he said or did. I believe Lord Lin Fang forgot whom he was addressing. Father is a reincarnation of the god, Buddha, and Silla is the Pure Land paradise of our eternal afterlife. Surely, the Buddha outranks the Son of Heaven.

At long last, Lord Lin Fang handed Father the official Sui calendar. Father compared it against our own as a formality, for our native astronomers are every bit as accomplished as those in China. Slowly a frown pulled his dark beard downward.

"I see a discrepancy," Father said. "The Chinese calendar predicts an eclipse of the sun on the first day of the tenth month."

Our royal astronomers rushed forward in alarm. As you know, Grandmother, an eclipse is a very serious matter, and the king must prepare rituals to fight it. But at the same time, if he makes a ritual, and the sun is not swallowed, he will look very foolish before his people. Astronomers have been put to death for wrong predictions.

"The Son of Heaven's calendar is accurate," said Lord Lin Fang imperiously.

"We will recheck our calculations, Ambassador," the chief astronomer stammered. I could tell from his shaking voice, he feared to contradict so renowned a man as Lord Lin Fang.

All of this left my father in a very awkward position. Of course he wished to support his own astronomers, but at the same time, he did not wish to offend so powerful an ally.

"I will meditate on the matter and take it up with the *hwabaek*," he said at last, referring to our council of nobles.

With that we were dismissed, Grandmother. Lord Lin Fang barely glanced at me when he left the hall.

22nd day of the 11th moon, 16th year of King Chinp'yŏng

From out here on my stargazing spot, I can see the lanterns burning in the astronomers hall, where Father's men go over and over their calculations, looking for a mistake. I have been doing the same, Grandmother, but I cannot find one.

Sometimes I feel like the stars are members of my own family, Grandmother. They coexist, they sometimes fly at one another, they hold secrets, just like families. As I bow to Mother and Father each morning, so I bow each night to the four palaces of the sky.

The Blue-Green Dragon of the East
The Scarlet Bird of the South

The White Tiger of the West

The Black Tortoise of the North.

I have long studied these four palaces. They are divided into twenty-eight lunar mansions, like unequal slices of pie. Father's astronomers taught me the mansions are named after the important constellations located inside them, and represent the king, the queen, the generals, the court officials, and more. Everything on Earth has its counterpart in Heaven, Grandmother. There is the Celestial River, that milky wash of stars that fills the center of the sky. There are the nine stars that shine brighter than others in this river and there we say the water must be shallow. There are even silly stars like the constellation called the Heavenly Pigsty, and the four-star constellation called the Heavenly Outhouse!

But my favorite constellation of all, Grandmother, is the celestial timepiece, the Great Northern Dipper, called *Ch'ilsŏng*. The handle of *Ch'ilsŏng* turns one degree every night and so points due north in winter, due east in spring, due south in summer, and due west in autumn.

By reading the position of *Ch'ilsŏng*, we always know what day of the year it is. Even when I have trouble identifying the other constellations, I always recognize *Ch'ilsŏng*. You know, Grandmother, the northernmost star in its handle represents Father, the king. It is a constellation of great power.

Let me turn once more to my calculations, Grandmother, and see if I cannot find my mistake.

23rd day of the 11th moon, 16th year of King Chinp'yŏng

I have been thinking over my meeting with Lord Lin Fang, and I realize I must have done something to give the ambassador offense. Why else would he turn from me so coolly? I am sure once he learns of our shared love of the stars, we will have many long talks, just as I have with Father's court astronomers. I should approach him again, in a less formal setting, do you not agree, Grandmother?

24th day of the 11th moon, 16th year of King Chinp'yŏng

Well, Grandmother, any hope I had of forming a friendship with Lord Lin Fang has crumbled to dust.

I think he was quite startled to find me at his door this

morning, since I had not thought to ask permission to see him, nor to send word I was coming. As heir to the throne, everyone in Silla is honored to have me pay a visit, and I assumed the ambassador would be, too.

His Chinese servants ushered me in nervously. Lord Lin Fang sat behind a heavy wooden desk, perched on an intricately carved chair that he had brought with him from the Sui court. Astronomer's tools lay on the desk, and I noticed he had a chart for calculating the phases of the moon. He rose and bowed slightly to me, but did not offer me a place to sit nor any refreshment.

I barely noticed his cool reception at the time, Grandmother. Without any ceremony or formal greetings, I launched right in on my theories about the eclipse. The longer I talked, the higher his eyebrows seemed to raise, until I feared they might fly off his face in alarm. I spoke to him as a fellow lover of astronomy, as one who sought the truth above all other things. He did not interrupt me, but let me go on with my calculations and theories. A solar eclipse comes only once in eighteen years, eleven and one-third months, I said. It can only fall during a new moon. Someone must have miscalculated a leap month, and that is where the discrepancy lies. I was speaking quickly, and I felt my voice creep higher and louder with excitement, until at last I finished in a rush of breath, saying, "And that is why our astronomers are correct, while the Son of Heaven's must by necessity be wrong."

Hearing the words out of my mouth, I immediately felt them to be undiplomatic, but once said, they could not be taken back.

"I am happy to advise your father's astronomers, and you may tell them so, Lady Sŏndŏk," Lord Lin Fang said frigidly. "But surely you cannot imagine I would converse on such a serious subject with a young lady? It would be unnatural, and wholly against the laws of propriety."

The laws of propriety? I knew the Confucians took their codes of behavior very seriously, but I thought with some certainty that these would not extend to a foreign princess and fellow lover of astronomy. Lin Fang's face showed me I was very much mistaken in my assumption of friendship. Under his gaze, I felt like the tiniest, lowliest bug. Hastily, I apologized for disturbing him and scuttled back to my room.

26th day of the 11th moon,
16th year of King Chinp'yŏng

Two days have passed, yet I am still so troubled by my interview with the ambassador. Are we not both interested in understanding the mysteries of the universe? Should not our shared passion excuse my minor breech of formality? Can Lord Lin Fang truly be so rigid? He has made me feel ashamed of my natural impulses.

28th day of the 11th moon, 16th year of King Chinp'yŏng

I have just heard word that the ambassador will return to China after the New Year's celebrations. I must admit to being relieved. Only a month before he is gone, and then things can get back to normal.

1st day of the 12th moon, 16th year of King Chinp'yŏng Sohan (Little Cold)

Why they call this day "Little Cold" I will never know. It is always bitterly windy and almost always snowing. We have drifts up to my hips and all the hunters are strapping on snowshoes.

At least the palace is lovely. All twenty-one official buildings are frosted white. Our servants make tiny blue footprints as they scurry from hall to hall, avoiding the long, snarling-fang icicles that hang from the eaves and constantly threaten to break upon their heads. Puffs of breath wreathe around the guards manning each of the eight gates. Puffs of smoke rise from the kitchen. When I was a child, I used to beg treats from the head cook, and I still find comfort at her open hearth, and in the comfortable clutter of hanging tables and pots.

I wish I had someone interesting to talk to. My sisters are utterly happy to sew and play music, and my waiting women have more in common with my sisters than with me. I have heard Chajang and the *hwarang* are off at Hwangyǒng Monastery looking for Enlightenment. Sometimes, I feel so out of place here, Grandmother. It makes my disappointment with Lord Lin Fang as bitter as the weather.

5th day of the 12th moon, 16th year of King Chinp'yǒng

The wild geese are flying home, Grandmother.

This means there is less than a month until the New Year and the beginning of spring. We have only one moon of ice and snow to pass through. Today there was a great crowd of magistrates and peasants in the courtyard, come to pay their taxes in rice and barley, but we women were tucked safe inside, sewing New Year's garments.

While we were bent over our needlework, I told Mother about my encounter with Lin Fang. When I was finished, Mother sighed and told me I had very bad manners.

"Why should you scold me?" I asked her. "It was the ambassador who was rude. Imagine speaking that way to the heir of Silla. No one at this court would dare to speak so."

"Lord Lin Fang simply finds it unimaginable a woman could rule," Mother answered, never taking her eyes off her fine stitching. "It is not surprising. No woman has ever ruled in her own right. Not here. Nor in Paekche or Koguryŏ. Nor in China, either."

"Grandmother ruled for Father," I shot back. "It is traditional here for a mother to govern for her underage child when his father dies. It is traditional in China, too. Is it not?"

"But only from behind the screen," Mother rejoined mildly. "Queen mothers sit behind the throne and hide themselves from view, so that they might not be seen. In China, they believe a woman must not leave the inner rooms of the palace, much less become a public figure. And a mother must only rule for her son, never for herself."

"Well, I shall rule well, and out in the open. What sort of queen should I be to hide myself from my people?"

"Do not alienate your father's strongest ally, Daughter," Mother said, and I saw she had stitched a lovely hem of peonies, while my thread was all tangles and knots. "Or you may find yourself with no people left to rule."

7th day of the 12th moon,
16th year of King Chinp'yŏng

The worst thing happened today, Grandmother. An enormous icicle fell from the roof with a shattering crash and landed beside one of Mother's ladies-in-waiting. It did not strike her, but the sound was so terrifying that she fell to the ground in a dead faint and has not awakened. The other ladies are saying that the sound startled one of her souls and caused it to fly away — that is why she remains asleep. Our doctors believe her *um* and *yang* are out of balance, and that she must have too much dark, feminine *um* influence.

9th day of the 12th moon, 16th year of King Chinp'yŏng

My mother's waiting woman has not regained consciousness, and her family has just sent for a *mudang*. Most people of the court rely on Chinese remedies, but when a member of the family is really ill, they fall back on old beliefs.

From your days on Earth, I am sure you remember these shaman priestesses, relics of our kingdom before we found the Way of the Buddha. Some of Silla's earliest kings were even shamans like the *mudang*. But now we have been civilized by the Buddha, and I no longer see the need for their ceremonies, or *kuts*. The ritual has not changed, Grandmother. First, the woman comes, dressed in layers of brightly dyed *chima*. Then the wailing and singing and shaking of rattles begins. Then the different ancestors and gods take possession of the *mudang* and make her speak in strange voices. It is terrifying to watch. Yet, people still believe the *mudang* have the power to drive away evil influences and invite good health to enter the person sponsoring the *kut*. I suppose there is always a chance you will want to come back in a *kut*, Grandmother. If so, I hope you will be benevolent and not demand so much food and money as the other greedy spirits do.

Since Father is a reincarnation of the Buddha, he has little use for these women, but he recognizes that others still believe. Whenever they fall into one of their trances or spirit possessions, speaking in the voice of an angry god, my blood freezes in my body. I know the common people depend on the *mudang* to drive away illness and to tell fortunes, but if it were up to me, I would banish them all.

10th day of the 12th moon, 16th year of King Chinp'yŏng

The *mudang* attributes Mother's waiting woman's illness to ancestral displeasure. The woman's family has not sponsored a *kut* in several years, and her forefathers and mothers are hungry and bored. My sisters and I peeked into the room where a feast was spread for the unhappy ancestors, and where the shaman priestess was singing and calling down the spirits. Sŏnwha was fascinated, but I wanted to run away. I would never want to be possessed by a spirit the way these women are. They became violent, irrational, and utterly out of control. I could not stand to lose control of myself that way, Grandmother.

12th day of the 12th moon, 16th year of King Chinp'yŏng

The *mudang*'s *kut* lasted two days, but yesterday, Mother's waiting woman awoke. The shamaness congratulated herself, but I noticed doctors were also in attendance, giving the sick woman herbs and elixirs. Who is to say what roused her from her slumber? Did her soul return? Or would she have recovered with no intervention at all?

13th day of the 12th moon, 16th year of King Chinp'yŏng

I have displeased Father.

We three daughters were called in to play upon our *kayagum*, when Father was entertaining Lord Lin Fang and some other visitors, last night after our meal. Ch'ŏnmyong and Sŏnwha moved their fingers delicately over the strings, but I made many mistakes, jarring my listeners and causing my father to frown. To speak truthfully, I haven't been practicing much recently because I have been refining my theory as to how the Chinese astronomers could have been mistaken about the eclipse.

Even as I was playing, my head was full of stars and angles and tables of figures.

When we finished playing, Father praised Ch'ŏn-myong and Sŏnwha, but said not a word to me. I saw a meaningful glance pass between Lin Fang and one of the other guests. Surely Father does not care about something so trivial as a lackluster *kayagum* concert. I had the astronomical fate of his kingdom on my mind.

15th day of the 12th moon,
16th year of King Chinp'yŏng
Taehan (Greater Cold)

Of course the day we call Greater Cold is mild by comparison with the day we call Little Cold. Because the weather was bright and sunny, I was walking down by the lake when I spotted Lord Lin Fang walking on the other side, absorbed in a book by Confucius. Mother had made me thoroughly ashamed of my bad manners, and Father's displeasure with me last night had left me contrite. I should not alienate Father's ally, I thought. Maybe it was possible to make amends for my earlier brashness.

I overtook the ambassador, who looked up with surprise from his reading. With a low bow, I begged his forgiveness.

"I believe we have gotten off to a bad start, Ambassador," I said, swallowing my pride. "It would give me the greatest pleasure to learn the workings of the stars from one of your fame. I humbly ask you to teach me the ways of the glorious astronomers in China, so that I might learn from those of greater wisdom."

"Lady Sŏndŏk," said the ambassador with a look so puckered he might have just tasted an unripe persimmon. "As I have told you before, astronomy is not the proper adornment for a young lady. A woman interested in the stars is like a fish interested in the treetops — it is a dangerous, unnatural place for her to be. A young lady should adorn herself with jewelry and children, and leave science to those whose minds are best equipped for it."

I felt slapped across the face by his words, Grandmother. I had tried three times to engage this awful man, but he would have none of my friendship.

"If I am to rule in Silla, I must understand what the heavens desire of me," I said, trying to explain the importance of my pursuit. "I must take care not to unbalance the universe."

"If you were to become queen, Heaven would be

turned on its head," Lin Fang said coldly. "I cannot imagine the gods will allow a woman to rule in her own right."

I could not think of anything cutting enough to say to this man, Grandmother. I turned stiffly and left him without another word. Luckily, I held my tears until I reached my own rooms. At least I did not cry like a child in front of the haughty Lin Fang.

18th day of the 12th moon, 16th year of King Chinp'yŏng

Buddha be praised, the *hwarang* have returned from their monastery retreat. Chajang is back and I will have someone of sense to talk to.

20th day of the 12th moon, 16th year of King Chinp'yŏng

I had a long talk with my friend Chajang this afternoon, and I realized how far I have to go on my path to Enlightenment. I was complaining about Lord Lin Fang's arrogance and how badly he made me feel.

"Why does he look down upon me?" I demanded of my friend. "Why cannot he treat me like an equal, deserving of respect?"

"Why let him bother you?" asked Chajang, who had just come from the temple at Hwangyŏng and was full of the Buddha's wisdom.

"I cannot help it. I had hoped to learn so much from him, but he thinks I am just a silly little girl, too far beneath him to teach."

"If humans could just eliminate their desires," he replied, "there would be no more suffering. If you practiced detachment, as the Buddha did, and cared not what Lin Fang thought of you, he would lose his power to make you angry." He smiled at me mischievously and said, "Our desires are our downfall, Lady Sŏndŏk."

Chajang is right, and if I were a true daughter of the Buddha, I would practice detachment. But how can I, Grandmother, when Lin Fang is such a vexing person?

27th day of the last moon,
16th year of King Chinp'yŏng

I have thought over what Chajang said and realized he is correct. The ambassador is scheduled to depart soon, anyway, and surely I can tolerate his presence for a few more weeks. After all, who wants to think of sour old men when the New Year is approaching? Lord Lin Fang will be swept away with the rest of last year's bad luck. Good riddance I say!

Last day of the last moon, 16th year of King Chinp'yŏng

All the servants are racing around cleaning the halls from top to bottom. Remember, Grandmother, for the first five days of the New Year they are not allowed to use a broom or they might sweep away our good fortune. From lowest to highest we are making new clothes in which to greet the New Year. We must all bathe our hair tonight, too, so that we won't wash away luck in the New Year.

Tonight we will sit down with all of our relatives and feast in honor of you, Grandmother. And Grandfather, and all of our Kim ancestors.

With no moon in the sky, the heavens are lit only by the milky net of stars. You know how deeply I wish for my own observatory as a New Year's present, Grandmother. Please whisper in Father's ear.

1st day of the 1st moon,
17th year of King Chinp'yŏng
Ipch'un (Spring Begins)

Happy Year of the Rabbit, Grandmother!

I have just returned from performing the *saebae* bow before my parents, and now I bow low to you, Grandmother. We are off to tidy your grave and present you and Grandfather with your New Year's meal. The cooks have prepared more than fifty dishes for you this year. I hope you are hungry.

Later

The festival at Half-moon Fortress was the most elaborate I can remember. All the adults of lesser rank wore their best clothes, with bright, new, wide-sleeved *chogori,* while the children ran around in their happiest colors. We of the royal Holy Bone rank were bedecked in the most costly new clothing — Father in new purple robes, Mother and the girls and I in richly embroidered red silk. I wore my golden shoes (which hurt my feet terribly!) and my beaten gold crown designed to resemble reindeer antlers, which tinkles musically when I walk. I am happy not to have to dress so every day. I was so weighted down with gold rings on every finger and toe, I could barely move.

The court musicians performed their slow and stately dances, but I wandered off to see the peasants' celebration, which was taking place just outside the palace walls. The farmers leaped and sang, beating drums and playing upon pipes. I sometimes yearn to sing and dance along with the common people, Grandmother. It looks like such wonderful sport. But as Chajang says, "Desires are our downfall," so I try not to wish too hard.

My seven-year-old cousin, Chindŏk, was more excited than I had ever seen her. She jumped upon the seesaw with other young girls of her rank, flying high into the air, and landing hard on her end. They squealed and flew, each jumping harder to send the other soaring. I would have loved to play at seesaw, but in this ceremonial costume, I would have landed like a bag of rocks.

2nd day of the 1st moon,
17th year of King Chinp'yŏng

We went to bed last night after feasting on our special New Year's *tuk-tuk,* which every person in Silla, from prince to peasant, eats on this day. It is made from steamed sticky rice, pounded and cut into the shape of coins and half-moons. The soup is stewed with beef and soy sauce and thinly sliced eggs. And as you recall, Grandmother, many say you will not age a year unless you drink this soup. I drank mine and turned fifteen this year. Ch'ŏn-myong turned fourteen, and Sŏnwha thirteen.

We also played a prank on Sŏnwha. Old legends say that a ghost descends the first night of the New Year and tries on every shoe he can find. When he finds one that fits, he steals it and the person who loses a shoe has bad luck all year. Sŏnwha forgot to hide her shoes when she went to bed. So Ch'ŏn-myong and I took one, and when Sŏnwha woke this morning, we told her the ghost had been to visit her. We felt guilty when she burst into tears, and so decided to give back the shoe. The strangest thing is, Grandmother, that when I went to get it from the chest where I had hidden it, the shoe was no longer there. I gave her one of my shoes to stop her crying, but now I don't know who has the bad luck — her with two mismatched shoes, or me with only one.

Our family went out among our people, who dropped to their knees and touched their heads to the ground when we passed. Mother, the girls, and I rode in our chariot, which only queens and aristocrats of the highest rank are allowed to do. Whenever we dismounted, our servants laid down a river of silk for us to tread upon.

From behind stone walls, our city's black-tiled houses rose gracefully, their flaring roofs looked ready to fly away. While only we of the Holy Bone rank might use the five sacred colors — red, black, white, yellow, and green — to paint our palaces, the natural wood of these houses is still beautiful. Grandmother, you will be happy to know that Kumsŏng does not have the crowded, poor hovels you find elsewhere. We have passed a law that the walls of a city house should be three times as tall as the average man, so that the people are not cramped inside breathing un-healthy air.

Our procession stopped at one of the large markets where merchants from the far west bring their wares. Every shape of man trades things here — men from China and Samarkand and India and Yamato Japan. There are more Arab merchants than ever, Grandmother. You wouldn't believe the things they bring back from their strange lands. In return for the silk and spices we provide, they bring glass and beads and strong, fast horses. One merchant with a thick black beard led a caravan of camels down the street. They are so common now, no one even gives them a second glance.

Our procession took us past a house where an old *mudang* was holding a *kut* before a huge crowd. This particular old woman did not bow low to the ground like the court-appointed shaman who attended Mother's waiting woman, but brazenly looked us in the eye as we passed. She was missing her upper teeth and her lower ones were black with decay. She had a crazed look about her, Grandmother, like one who has seen far too much for one lifetime and has been ruined by it.

"She is a very powerful shamaness," one of Mother's ladies-in-waiting said. "They say the god *Ch'ilsŏng* possesses her and always speaks true."

"May we stop and see her, Mother?" Sŏnwha begged. "Please?"

But Mother had a strange, troubled look on her face and told us we must hurry along. The *mudang* continued to follow Mother with her unsettling eyes until, at last, we turned the corner and rode out of view.

Later

Sŏnwha was so eager to have her fortune told, that at last, after much pleading and whining, she prevailed upon Mother to let us return. Toward the end of the day, just before the sun was setting, our entourage made its way back to the *mudang*'s street. She was outside in the courtyard as if she had been waiting for us.

"I am exhausted from the *kut*," she said, in answer to our request for a fortune-telling. "It has been going on for three days. But for the royal family, I will try to once more invoke the god."

She spread out her mat and closed her eyes to get in touch with her personal spirit god, then cast her *yut* sticks three times with a violent gesture, taking me by surprise. They fell in a three-one-four pattern.

"Throw Jewel in River," she rasped, looking at Sŏnwha.

"What is that supposed to mean?" Sŏnwha demanded. "Will I lose my favorite necklace this year?" But the *mudang* did not answer. "Is a sacrifice expected of me? I am not going to throw my precious stones away," Sŏnwha cried. The *mudang* merely stared until my sister grew uncomfortable and stormed away. Next, the old diviner cast my sticks. They fell one-four-one.

"Tree Without Roots," the old woman said with a knowing look. I was as baffled by my fortune as Sŏnwha was by hers. What could that possibly mean? I opened my mouth to ask, but she was already casting the sticks for Mother. They fell three-four-one, which she announced meant "Traveler Thinks of Home." When she looked at Mother, the old *mudang*'s expression turned from annoyance to one of confusion. She picked up the sticks and cast them again, but once more they fell in the three-four-one pattern. So sadly did the old woman gaze upon my mother then, that I immediately grew concerned. Mother stared at the sticks and then at the old woman, and it seemed to me a whole conversation passed between them, spoken only by their eyes. I tried to ask the *mudang* what Mother's fortune meant — she never travels anywhere except when we are all with her — but the old woman hurriedly gathered her sticks, folded her cloth, and stalked back into her house. I think this old fortune-teller is a fraud, Grandmother, and very foolish to cast such ill fortunes for the royal family. Tree without roots, indeed. What a way to begin the New Year!

10th day of the 1st moon,
17th year of King Chinp'yŏng

It is the Hour of the Pig when the whole palace is settling down to sleep and only the watchmen and astronomers are awake. I have not had a chance during the festival season to sit at my favorite stargazing spot. It is here where I feel most alive. Here inside the grand mystery of the stars.

This is the Year of the Rabbit, Grandmother, which is very favorable to astronomers because the rabbit lives in the moon. Those born in a Rabbit year are sensitive and loyal and prone to cry easily. The very wise philosopher, Master Confucius, was born in a Rabbit year, but I have a hard time imagining him weeping like a sentimental girl!

Surely, when Father was at your knee, you must have told him the story of how the astrological signs got their names. He used to tell me the story when I was but a little girl. He said on the day before Buddha left this Earth, he desired to see all the animals of the world. Only twelve showed up. They were the rat, ox, tiger, hare, dragon, snake, horse, sheep, monkey, fowl, dog, and pig. They ran a race to see in which order they would guard the astrological signs, and Ox was ahead. But the wily rat rode on his back, and at the last minute leaped over the finish line to become the first sign of the year. Buddha rewarded these faithful animals by assigning each an hour of the day.

The New Year's celebration is almost over, and I have not received the present I so greatly desire, Grandmother — an observatory. If only Father did not disapprove of my studying astronomy! He treats me as a son in many respects, but he seems more convinced than ever that the important business of charting the heavens should be left to men.

How can I help myself, Grandmother? During the day, everything is chaotic in Kumsŏng. Men rush around the palace, merchants hawk their wares. The city is a jumble of oxen and horses and children and slaves, all bellowing and laughing and tripping over one another to get where they are going. But at night, all is still and peaceful. I may look up into the heavens and find order.

The moon is waxing toward full and with the first full moon comes the end of our New Year's festival. Sometimes when I look up into the stars, I feel the patterns resolve themselves in pictures, and then it is almost as if I were staring at a painted scroll. At times like that, I feel I can see the future as clearly as any old woman with her *yut* sticks.

That old *mudang* does not know of what she speaks. My roots are here, Grandmother. My roots are in the stars.

14th day of the 1st moon,
17th year of King Chinp'yŏng

Boys from all over the city are gathering sticks to build bonfires to greet the first full moon. I am determined to stay up all night with my elders and not fall asleep like a child.

15th day of the 1st moon,
17th year of King Chinp'yŏng
Usu (Season of First Rains)

I made it! This year I stayed up all night, Grandmother, and did not shut my eyes once until daybreak. Before, when I was young, I would drift off and all sorts of jokes would be played on me. This year, Ch'ŏn-myong could not keep awake. Sŏnwha and I dusted her eyebrows with rice flour and when Ch'ŏn-myong woke up, she screamed. She thought her eyebrows had turned white, which is what they say happens to people who fall asleep on the night before the first full moon. We followed the tradition of the Lucky Nines all day, performing every task nine times for good luck. I washed my face nine times and brushed my teeth with salt nine times. I bowed nine times before you, Grandmother, and washed the white rice I placed inside you in nine bowls of freshwater.

I am being called to go to the ancestral shrine, Grandmother. I will write more later. Good-bye, good-bye, good-bye, good-bye, good-bye, good-bye, good-bye, good-bye, good-bye.

Later

We have just returned from Hwangyŏng Monastery, where we laid our offerings before the Three Spirits: *Sanshin*, who is represented as an old man with a tiger, *Toksŏng*, the lone spirit, who is a solitary scholar, and *Ch'ilsŏng*, my favorite, the Seven-star spirit of the Great Northern Dipper. As the daughter of the reincarnated Buddha, I must take my religious observances very seriously. I prayed for the one present that is my heart's desire. Will Father grant it to me?

Later still

Just as we were preparing to go to bed, Father called Ch'ŏn-myong, Sŏnwha, and me outside for one last New

Year's surprise. He led us to the royal stables, where he keeps nearly 20,000 horses, and told us to close our eyes and wish very hard for something lovely. As I stood with my eyes closed, I heard very soft snorting and the prancing hooves of something small, too small to be a horse. Sŏnwha opened her eyes before Father told us we might, and squealed with delight. Grandmother, there stood three of the smallest horses I'd ever seen! Father explained that these miniature creatures were called *kwaha*, or "under-fruit horses." They are so small, they can pass under fruit tree branches without touching them. I named my dear, sweet *kwaha* Moonbeam, because she is the same bright silvery color as the moon.

As the other girls ran to embrace their pets, Father took me aside. He had another present for his eldest daughter, he said. My heart leaped at his words, Grandmother. Finally, he would grant my desire.

"It is not an observatory," he said, as I unwrapped a small red package. Inside was a lovely golden bracelet, hung with the astrological signs — rat, ox, dragon, snake, horse, and so on — carved in jade. "But jewelry is a more fitting adornment for a young lady than astronomy."

I smiled weakly, trying to hide my disappointment, and returned with my giggling sisters to our chambers.

What concerns me most, Grandmother, is how suspiciously similar Father's words sounded to those of Lord Lin Fang's. Could the ambassador have had a hand in turning my father's mind?

16th day of the 1st moon, 17th year of King Chinp'yŏng

I am such an ungrateful child, Grandmother. I have everything a princess could want, and yet I am not happy. But it makes sense to have an observatory, one centralized location devoted only to stargazing. Right now, the astronomers work from their halls all over the kingdom, but there is no one place from which all measurements might be taken, no one holy spot devoted solely to the mapping of the heavens. Every year I ask for the same thing — an observatory of my very own, and every year my Father pats my head like a child. Before I was a child, but I have been working so hard this past year. I felt he was on the verge of giving in, Grandmother, but something changed.

Desires are our downfall. Desires are our downfall.

17th day of the 1st moon, 17th year of King Chinp'yŏng

The old saying "three days cold, four days warm" has never been more true. The last four days were mild, but we had anticipated spring too soon. Like a thief, winter has snuck back into the kingdom and stolen the sun. We have put on our quilted clothes again and sit inside watching the snow drift on the hipped roofs.

Today, Father called a meeting of the *hwabaek*. The meetings usually take place out of doors, under a tree on one of our holy mountains, but because of the snow, today we were inside. By the time I arrived and left my wet shoes on the porch, most of the ministers were already seated. Father sat under his richly embroidered canopy on silken pillows over the warm *ondal* floor. I took the pillow next to him as the highest-ranking member of the Holy Bone. Members of the aristocratic True Bone rank sat beyond us, and then the lower-ranking officials beyond them. I saw Chajang in the crowd and smiled at him. I saw almost nothing of him during the New Year's celebration.

There was much droning on of business, which I attended to as best I could. Father spoke of the Paekche troops gathering at our borders, and of the alliance our neighbors had formed against us. The *hwabaek* took a vote on whether or not to send troops to engage them, and after much wrangling came to a consensus. Lin Fang looked quizzically at Father, and Father had to explain that unlike China, the king is not the only voice in Silla. Here, our laws require us to have a unanimous decision among the nobles before we enact any important law. As far as I know, we are different from all other kingdoms in that way.

When at last the talk of war was done, Father made a pronouncement on the official calendar. His decision was so disappointing, Grandmother. He chose to override our calendar and substitute the Sui Emperor's with its predicted eclipse on the first day of the tenth month.

Though I am heir to the throne, in light of my sex, I am usually silent at these meetings. Today, however, I could not help but speak.

"Father, give me permission to address you," I bowed.

He appeared surprised, but nodded his head.

"I, too, have calculated the phases of the sun and moon, independently of your astronomers, and I must agree with them." I paused and rolled out the star chart I had secreted in my wide sleeve. "I presented my findings to Lord Lin Fang, and though he would not be persuaded, I must insist. It is mathematically impossible to have an eclipse in the tenth month of this year. I would not want my honorable father to trouble his mind."

Father's head astronomer sputtered and coughed. "I beg the Lady Sŏndŏk's pardon —" He tried to cover for me, but I was ready to reveal my secret.

"Sŏndŏk, I ordered you to give up stargazing," Father said.

"You did, Father. But I thought for the good of the kingdom —"

"I tried to tell the Lady Sŏndŏk that astronomy is a difficult science," Lord Lin Fang suddenly interjected, and his voice was thick and icy like the weather outside. "It should not be entrusted to a woman."

"Sŏndŏk fancies herself an astronomer," said Father, casting an annoyed look my way. "She is a clever girl, but sometimes she oversteps her place."

"Where I come from," Lin Fang stated, "we believe a woman is ruled by her father in childhood, by her husband in adulthood, and by her son in old age. A woman does not venture to voice her own opinion."

"I am aware of what you believe in China, sir," I interrupted and saw the ambassador's curly eyebrows shoot up. I spoke as politely as I could, though my fury with this wretched man threatened to choke me. "But we are not in China. Nor are we in Koguryŏ or Paekche, who also believe as you do. We are in Silla. And here a woman may speak her mind, and inherit property, and even ascend to the throne, as I am to do. It is a person's bone rank, not her sex, that determines these matters."

I had gone too far. I could immediately tell by the anger in my father's voice.

"I fear our women are far less well-mannered than what you are used to at home," Father said, refusing to look at me. "Sŏndŏk, return to your rooms now and practice your *kayagum*. You may perform for me after dinner."

I gathered up my charts in dismay and anger, Grandmother. To be dismissed and ordered to practice my music like a useless girl! As I stormed out, I caught Chajang's eyes, which were full of pity. He was the only one with enough courage to look at me.

Later

It is the Hour of the Rat, and I should be in bed, but I am still so angry with Father and Lord Lin Fang.

I am sitting upon the ledge of the mountain, wrapped in furs, and writing by lantern light. Why should women be denied the stars?

I <u>will</u> learn to read the stars well and I <u>will</u> understand them. I am sure I shall become a great ruler, Grandmother. As great a ruler as any Holy Bone rank king before me.

It has begun to snow again. I must return to my chamber.

*18th day of the 1st moon,
17th year of King Chinp'yŏng*

I am so furious I could break that infernal *kayagum* into a thousand pieces! I sought an audience with Father today, to try and once more persuade him that my calculations were correct. I found him holding an audience with Lord Lin Fang.

"Practice your playing, Sŏndŏk. Help your mother with the silkworms. Work on your weaving, daughter," was all he said. And that cadaverous old ambassador just smirked, as if I were nothing but a silly little girl playing with dolls. The ambassador nodded approvingly.

Thank the Buddha he is going home soon.

23rd day of the 1st moon, 17th year of King Chinp'yŏng

Abominable news today, Grandmother. Father has engaged Lin Fang as our tutor! With Paekche threatening our borders, Father thought it would be a wise stratagem to have the ambassador stay on.

I told Father that I had already asked Lin Fang to instruct me, and that he had refused.

"I am not having him teach you astronomy, daughter. I want him to guide you in the laws of Confucius."

"Confucius?" I cried. "Father, we have customs of our own. We don't need the rigid laws of Confucius."

"Your forwardness at the *hwaebek* showed me I have been too indulgent with you," Father said sternly. "If you are to be my heir, you need to conduct yourself in a manner other countries will respect. You need to appreciate their beliefs."

There were many paths a man might walk in life, Father explained, and the Way of the Buddha encourages us to take the best of every philosophy we encounter, and — equally important — to be closed-minded about none. Many great things have come to us from the land of Confucius. "Including your stars, if I'm not mistaken," he said.

I could not argue, for all the earliest writings on the heavens came to us from our neighbor to the north.

"Sŏndŏk," Father continued when I remained silent. "We are a small and isolated kingdom. We may one day have need of China to devour our enemies."

"But what if we are devoured in return?" I asked.

"What better way to avoid that than to learn how they play their game? Pay attention to the lessons Lin Fang teaches you," said Father, waving his hand to dismiss me. "An ignorant queen is a conquered queen."

25th day of the 1st moon, 17th year of King Chinp'yŏng

My sisters are furious with me. They have to sit with me while Lord Lin Fang instructs us on the finer points of Chinese writing and teaches us histories of men they care nothing about. Neither catches on as quickly as I do and Lin Fang is very cross with them. But even when I give every answer correctly, even when my calligraphy is formed perfectly, he still saves a special frown just for me.

Lord Lin Fang seems no more excited about teaching a roomful of girls than we are in learning from him. We sit at our low tables with our ink sticks and brushes, our faces turned up to him like spring flowers to the sun. But such a cold winter sun he is, Grandmother. Scowling and sighing. We are to read the Five Classic texts. We are to study philosophy and poetry and the sayings of Master Confucius. When I asked him if we were to study astronomy as well, he turned stonily away from me, refusing to dignify such a silly question with an answer.

26th day of the 1st moon, 17th year of King Chinp'yŏng

Today, Lin Fang taught us about the Five Confucian Relationships. They are:

Affection between father and son
Justice between ruler and subject
Obedience of wife to husband
Precedence between elder and younger, and
Trust between friends.

Interestingly enough, there is no mention of daughters.

1st day of the 2nd moon,
17th year of King Chinp'yŏng
Kyŏngch'ip (Hibernating Creatures Awake)

There are no lessons this morning in honor of Slaves' Day. All the peasants and farmers lay down their burdens and relax before planting season. I hope you enjoy the fresh rice I have placed in you today, Grandmother. I hope that you will see fit to help me in my struggles against the abominable Lin Fang.

The *mudang* are up to their old tricks again. I think they are an embarrassment, and Father should forbid them from practicing their offensive arts. The old woman who told our fortunes on New Year's Day was outside the palace gates, on the other side of the South Stream. Sŏnwha dragged me over the Moon Spirit Bridge to watch the *kut* she was performing. She was dancing with bare feet on the blade of a knife and doing no injury to herself. The crowd around her was wild with delirium, shouting and dancing to the rhythm of her ceremonial drum.

"That sort of behavior should be outlawed," said Lin Fang, referring to the old *mudang*, who had set down her blades and was now going around in the guise of a god extorting gifts from all the onlookers.

What a surprise, Grandmother. At last, Lin Fang and I have found something on which we can agree.

4th day of the 2nd moon,
17th year of King Chinp'yŏng

Back to our classwork. Lord Lin Fang is teaching us from the *Book of Rites*. Today's lesson was on the Seven Evils, or the seven reasons a man may set aside his wife. These are:

Stealing

Jealousy

Carrying a hereditary disease

Committing adultery

Being disrespectful to one's mother-in-law

Talking too much

Failure to bear a son

He looked pointedly at Sŏnwha when he spoke on the evils of talking too much, and at me when the topic turned toward bearing a son. I know he views our mother with distaste, as if she were but half a woman, less than nothing. In Lin Fang's eyes, she has utterly failed our father. Many of our ministers agree, and there was talk at one point about him taking a new wife. But Father loves Mother and would not hear of it. And besides, he has no need of a male heir. He has me.

Later

Oh, Grandmother, I am one of many proud words, but deep down I am so afraid. There has never been a queen of Silla. What if our enemies use my reign as an excuse to attack? What if the nobles rebel against a feminine head of state? What if my wretched body is the means by which our kingdom is destroyed? Sometimes I can hardly bear the strain, Grandmother, and I suffer such blinding headaches. Today, when I gave a wrong answer, Lin Fang seemed disgusted with me, and quoted Confucius saying, "Rotten wood cannot be sculpted. A manure wall cannot be plastered." What if he is right, Grandmother? What if I am simply not up to the task?

8th day of the 2nd moon,
17th year of King Chinp'yŏng

I am feeling a little better today and am ashamed of my coward's words. I do not honor you, Grandmother, when I doubt myself. I have redoubled my efforts at study.

Today was Excited Insect Day. The insects waking is one of the surest signs of spring. With all the buzzing and whirring, we could hardly hear ourselves talk, and Lin Fang dismissed us early.

The peach trees have just begun to blossom and the oriole sings in the pale green willow bough. Father's *hwarang* were practicing their archery in the palace courtyard.

Many talented young men were taking turns at the archery target. They galloped across the courtyard, their knees tightly hugging their horses' backs; loaded their bows, fired off five arrows in rapid succession. Only members of the Holy and True Bone ranks are recruited into the *hwarang*, and so I recognized almost everyone. Many of the most handsome young men were from my mother's Pak clan. There were others from the Paks' rival, the Sohn clan. Then in rode my friend Chajang, who put them all to shame. Each one of his five arrows struck the black square center and stuck there triumphantly. I could not help but cheer for him. He was magnificent.

Lin Fang stepped out of our schoolroom and stood watching the display with my sisters and me.

"What a fine specimen of a boy," he said, when Chajang rode by and bowed deeply to our royal party. "Such a shame he is not a king's son."

15th day of the 2nd moon,
17th year of King Chinp'yŏng
Ch'unbun (Spring Equinox)

I hung a small bell on my incense clock, and when the wick burned down to the correct place, the bell dropped into a small copper bowl next to my bed and woke me. It is late in the hour of the Ox, everyone has been asleep for hours. I am so very tired tonight, Grandmother. And yet I must go out and measure the stars, for today is *Ch'unbun,* the spring equinox. So here I am back on my rocky out-cropping with my instruments and lantern. Exhausted.

All day I work to understand the classic Chinese texts so that Lin Fang will not be able to reproach me. All night I measure the stars to understand their meaning for our kingdom. Then, it is back to the classroom where Lin Fang makes me feel like a witless child. I must not fail in front of that awful man. I am to be the first queen Silla has ever known. I must prove to him that I am as good as Chajang. No, I cannot just be good. I must be the

16th day of the 2nd moon, 17th year of King Chinp'yŏng

Such shame, Grandmother! I fell asleep outside last night while I was writing to you, and was discovered by one of Father's guards. He reported me this morning, and I was led before Father like a common thief caught stealing rice. "No more, Sŏndŏk!" Father boomed. "Enough stargazing. You may appreciate the moon for its brilliance and the stars for their fire, but I command you to leave the science to men. I will not tell you again."

What am I to do? Without the stars, I am hardly myself.

17th day of the 2nd moon, 17th year of King Chinp'yŏng

Sŏnwha does not understand, Grandmother. She daydreams in class and when Lin Fang shouts at her, she just shrugs and laughs. "Why do you care so much, Sŏndŏk?" she asks. "There are more things in the world than planets and books."

Sŏnwha can barely tell the sun from the moon! These days all she talks about is boys. She spends all day staring in the mirror, combing her hair and admiring her large, almond eyes. She will catch a husband soon and never have to think again.

Lin Fang was especially puffed up today. "I've heard you have laid down your instruments, Lady Sŏndŏk," he said. "Now you might have time to pick up a schoolbook." He should not challenge me this way.

18th day of the 2nd moon, 17th year of King Chinp'yŏng

My cousin, Chindŏk, is a sweet child, but she is driving me to distraction. She whines that I never play with her anymore, but I have so much to read if I am to show Lin Fang. Another headache today.

19th day of the 2nd moon, 17th year of King Chinp'yŏng

The language in *The Analects*, or *The Sayings*, of Confucius that Lin Fang assigned us is very difficult. I find myself reading the passages two and three times before they make any sense to me. Why can't I understand it quicker? Why is this so hard for me?

20th day of the 2nd moon, 17th year of King Chinp'yŏng

I woke up during the Hour of the Rat last night, and from my window I could see the waning moon was but a crescent, and the bright *um* planet *Kumsŏng* hung just below like a jewel. My first thought was to reach for my armillary sphere, but then I remembered Father's command. How does one disobey the reincarnated Buddha? I picked up *The Analects* instead and tried to read, but the moon kept pulling me back to the window.

Would it really be so bad to slip out for a moment and take a few quick measurements? So long as no one finds out, who have I really harmed?

Let this be our secret, Grandmother.

21st day of the 2nd moon, 17th year of King Chinp'yŏng

Today, Sŏnwha interrupted my studies to make me watch the *hwarang* go through their drills on the mountainside. "You work too hard, Sŏndŏk," she said. "You must allow yourself to relax." I argued, but at last she had her way. Indeed, I think the fresh air did me good, Grandmother, for I have lately been suffering bad headaches.

I rode my *kwaha*, Moonbeam, and Sŏnwha rode her Blossom to the steep slope behind Half-moon Fortress. There the *hwarang* were practicing their *tae kwon do*. This is the unarmed "foot fighting," if you remember, Grandmother, practiced by all *hwarang*. Sŏnwha pointed out Chajang, who kicked very gracefully.

"He's very handsome don't you think?"

"He is," I agreed.

"Tall and smart and a great lover of the Buddha."

"He is admirable," I replied.

"Sŏndŏk wants to marry Chajang!" she laughed. "Sŏndŏk is in love!"

Does my sister not realize when she talks like that she makes all girls look simpleminded and ridiculous? And, anyway, Chajang is a member of the True Bone rank. How could I, heir to the throne and member of the Holy Bone rank, even consider him?

Chajang saw us watching and walked over to us. "Lady Sŏndŏk," he said, bowing deeply. "Some of us are going hunting this afternoon. We would be most honored by your presence."

For some reason I felt very confused by his invitation,

Grandmother. My cheeks burned hotly. I told him it was impossible and hurriedly rode back to my studies.

22nd day of the 2nd moon, 17th year of King Chinp'yŏng

I have known Chajang all my life, Grandmother. We played together as children. I taught him the names of all the stars. He is just a silly little Herdboy.

So why did I blush when he spoke to me? I have gone as insane as an old *mudang*.

24th day of the 2nd moon, 17th year of King Chinp'yŏng

I actually found myself daydreaming in class today, Grandmother. Just like Sŏnwha! Lin Fang asked me a question about the Han Dynasty and I was remembering Chajang's long black hair swinging around as he kicked and felled his opponent. "Just as I suspected," Lin Fang said, when I stammered and begged him to repeat his question. "Just like all the rest." This will not do, Grandmother. This will not do.

25th day of the 2nd moon,
17th year of King Chinp'yŏng

Studied all day. Slipped outside and charted constellations all night. No thoughts of Chajang . . . until just now.

26th day of the 2nd moon,
17th year of King Chinp'yŏng

Studied. No thoughts.

1st day of the 3rd moon,
17th year of King Chinp'yŏng
Ch'ŏngmyŏng (Clear and Bright)

Today was *Hanshik*, the day where we may eat only cold food. I have never been completely sure why we do this, Grandmother. I have heard many stories, but my favorite is the most tragic. A long time ago, back when the tiger smoked his pipe, a faithful servant of a Chinese emperor was burned to death on this day. To honor this man, the emperor forbade the making of fires on the anniversary of his death forever after. For whatever reason, it is one of our most important and ancient festivals.

Today we bowed down before our ancestors and tidied their graves. I honored you, most sacred Grandmother, and our ancestors for four generations. We still believe the greatest of all misconducts is to neglect devotion and piety toward one's parents, living or dead.

Now back to my studies.

3rd day of the 3rd moon, 17th year of King Chinp'yŏng

Grandmother, I am hopelessly confused.

Today the weather was so warm and soft, our entire court went on an outing to the mountains. We settled by a rushing brook and ate the little rice cakes decorated with azalea leaves that belong to this day. I studiously avoided Chajang, who was sporting with some of the boys by the water. I was deeply absorbed in Confucius's *Analects,* and had no time for such horseplay.

"Your Majesty, tell the story of Sŏndŏk and the peonies!" Chindŏk begged my father, when we had eaten our feast and were resting afterward. I am always embarrassed when that story is told, for it shows me being a naughty, forward little girl, but Chindŏk loves it, because

I was the same age she is now when I was made my father's heir.

Father nestled Chindŏk on his knee, and put his other hand on my hair. When Father began to speak, all the courtiers drew near, and to my alarm, so did Chajang.

"Your cousin has always been the most clever girl I knew," Father began, causing me to blush immediately. "When she was but seven years old, the Emperor of China sent me a packet of peony seeds. We had never seen this flower before at court, and to show us what it would look like in full flower, the emperor sent along a painting.

"It showed three lovely, fat flowers in red, pink, and white. All the ladies and gentlemen of court were quite taken with the painting, and I placed the seeds in Sŏndŏk's chubby hand, saying, 'Look, little one, these seeds will one day become beautiful, perfumed flowers, like those that grow in the Emperor's private garden.'

"Well, Chindŏk," Father said, laughing at me over the little girl's head, "you should have seen the look of distress on your cousin's face. 'They are indeed beautiful,' she said with a little girl's absolute confidence. 'What a shame they will have no scent.'

(I blush to remember my own impertinence, Grandmother.)

"Of course this angered me," Father continued, frowning for Chindŏk's benefit. "'How can you possibly know the fragrance of these flowers will not equal their beauty?' I demanded. 'They are merely seeds.'

"'Surely, if the King of China had meant for you to appreciate the peonies' smell,' said Sŏndŏk boldly, 'he would have had them painted with bees and colorful butterflies attending. I mistrust the sweetness of a flower that the butterfly neglects.'

"Well, I had never heard anything so astute," Father laughed. "And from a child! I knew at that moment if the gods did not bless me with a son, clever Sŏndŏk would rule Silla after me. And it seems that is what the gods desire."

Father's voice trailed off and the lords and ladies sighed over Father's bad luck in siring nothing but daughters. I suddenly felt very foolish, like one who takes first prize in an archery contest because the best archer fails to show. Chajang noticed my distress and quickly approached us.

"If I may present a gift to fair Lady Chindŏk," he said, by way of breaking the silence. He had taken a reed of bamboo and fitted it with long grass for hair. Upon the reed, he had painted a tiny face, with round cheeks like Chindŏk's and a bright, happy smile.

"Please take this, beautiful lady, with your servant's humble regards," he bowed deeply to my cousin, but his eyes twinkled into mine.

Father noticed the exchange and looked startled. Hastily, I excused myself and reached for my *Analects*. Nothing hides a blush better than Master Confucius.

6th day of the 3rd moon, 17th year of King Chinp'yŏng

The silkworms are hatching and Mother makes us all tend them with her when we are done with our studies.

She has hundreds of ladies-in-waiting who might do the work, but the queen is expected to tend the silkworms to set a good example for the commoners. She enlists my sisters, and today I had to go, though I detest such ridiculous women's work. As if I didn't have enough studying to do! The Silkworm Hall is stiflingly hot, for there are lit braziers all around to warm the pupae. Thousands and thousands of small white creatures writhe upon trays while Mother feeds them hand-chopped mulberry leaves from her silken basket. This task must be repeated every half hour, day and night, until they spin their cocoons. Of course, Mother does not stay all night like the slaves, but the hours she puts in are exhausting. The tiny creatures are even greedier than the gods who possess the *mudang*, for they will eat enough to multiply their weight 10,000 times in the first month of their lives.

I entered the Silkworm Hall where the sound of so many jaws chewing was like heavy rain on a roof. Mother was in the back of the hall, chopping mulberry leaves with an iron blade. She is so delicate and lovely, she looks barely capable of lifting the knife, much less swinging it. Her long hair escaped its bun and she was singing a country ballad about a princess who was kidnapped by the Dragon King of the Sea. All in all, she looked more like a fresh peasant wife than a queen. I startled her with my approach.

"This is my favorite place in the fortress," Mother had to shout to be heard over the worms' jaws. "I would stay here all day, just dreaming and remembering happier times."

"Are you not happy, Mother?" I asked, for, to tell you the truth, Grandmother, I had never once given a thought to my mother's happiness beyond what duty required of me.

"With the war against Paekche heating up, I worry . . ." she began, but then cut herself off. She believes, like Lin Fang, that a woman should not make her opinions known. "There was a time when the hope of having a son was still alive," she said. "But now my body tells me otherwise."

"Mother," I answered, "you are still young. You —" She cut me off.

"Take up that basket of leaves," she ordered, dropping the topic completely. "These hungry creatures need to be fed."

8th day of the 3rd moon, 17th year of King Chinp'yŏng

When I appeared before Lin Fang for my lessons today, he dismissed me, saying, "The silkworms have need of you. Confucius would never want to stand in the way of a woman's duty to her worms."

He said it blandly, Grandmother, but deep down he was sneering at me. How can I take on the role of a scholar when I must tie up my hair and act a nursemaid to a million writhing worms?

9th day of the 3rd moon, 17th year of King Chinp'yŏng

In past years, I did not mind these duties, but now I feel like I want to scream. Chopping the feed, walking the rows, scattering the mulberry leaves: the endless, mind-numbing repetition of it. I recite the names of all the constellations in heaven to try to keep my mind limber, starting in the first Lunar Mansion and proceeding through the twenty-eighth. I sing them quietly to myself again and again. I hate this, Grandmother! I have far more important things to be doing.

I have such a headache.

10th day of the 3rd moon, 17th year of King Chinp'yŏng

Today Mother overheard me singing the 283 constellations and angrily gestured for me to be silent. These delicate, feeble, pampered creatures! They've reached the age when they can bear no loud noises beyond their own gluttony — no laughing, no talking, and, now, no humming even. We must protect them from harsh light and strong

70

smells. No smell of meat or fish. They can't even bear the aroma of human sweat. In this heat!

12th day of the 3rd moon, 17th year of King Chinp'yŏng

Oh, Grandmother, I am the worst of daughters.

I would blame it on exhaustion, only there can be no excuse. I was horrible to Mother and I richly deserve your scorn and the scorn of all my ancestors.

It all began because I was anxious to leave the Silkworm Hall and take a reading of the stars. I had been working all day — my shoulders ached and my head throbbed from the sound of the worms' chewing. I stepped out into the courtyard, and for the first time in three nights, the sky was perfectly clear and every star burned brightly. I wanted nothing more than to get my armillary sphere and take some measurements. But of course, I could not say that.

"Sŏndŏk." Mother ran after me. "You have one more feeding before you can retire. Come back inside."

Something snapped inside of me, Grandmother. I cannot describe it.

"I have more important things to do, Mother. Get one of your women to help you."

My mother was aghast. "Daughter, you know that royal women have always set an example by tending the silkworms. It is what queens have always done."

"Queens like you!" I shouted, having no care if I killed a thousand silkworms with the noise. "Queens who are nothing but an adornment and have no real business. But I have more important things to learn. I don't have time to waste on silkworms!"

My mother was horrified by my words, and turned away without answering me. At the time, I took her withdrawal as a great victory. Now I suspect it was nothing more than pity for how I would feel later.

So ashamed, Grandmother. So very ashamed.

Later

There is a red haze around the moon tonight, which bodes no good.

14th day of the 3rd moon, 17th year of King Chinp'yŏng

I know I should apologize to Mother, but I cannot bring myself to do it. I asked her permission to be readmitted to the Silkworm Hall, but she said I had better return to my studies. I was better off there. Ch'ŏn-myong would help her.

I don't know why I hate women's work so much, Grandmother. Logically, I know there is nothing shameful in it, but somehow I feel that if I do what is expected of me as a woman, I will lose the little, insecure foothold I have in the world of men. I sometimes feel torn between acting like a daughter to my mother and a son to my father. By nature, my flesh is weak, yet through my will I must toughen it to govern this kingdom upon my father's death. Maybe that *mudang* was right. I am a tree without roots.

15th day of the 3rd moon, 17th year of King Chinp'yŏng
Kok-woo (Grain Rains)

Father learned of my wicked behavior and I have been forbidden to leave my room except to study with Lin

Fang. I must sit here and meditate on my unfilial nature —
with no company, no treats, and certainly no stargazing.

And yet he cannot forbid me to look out of the window, Grandmother.

17th day of the 3rd moon, 17th year of King Chinp'yŏng

Grandmother, could my wickedness be causing me to lose
my sanity? Are the stars really so dangerous for me? I
have just had the most unsettling experience, and I don't
know how to describe it. It was so extraordinary, so terrifying, and yet I feel I will go mad if I do not tell someone.

I had spent the day locked in my room, thinking
about my unfilial nature. I finished the dinner my waiting women brought, and as night fell, I sat in my window
staring off into the heavens with an almost painful long-
ing. I know not how long I sat there, but after some time
the familiar constellation Brilliant Pearls, which lives inside the mansion called the Serving Woman seemed to
move in the sky — subtly at first, then boldly, like a character in a puppet show. As I watched, the stars resolved
themselves into the shape of a lovely woman. This woman
bowed to me, ablaze in her starry robe. I was astonished at

her beauty, and I knew, without knowing how I knew, that this creature was my mother. I watched for some minutes until, suddenly, star by star, she began to disappear. First, the stars of her shoulders and back were extinguished, then the stars of her thighs and feet, until gradually all that remained were two faint stars, like watchful eyes left behind. I blinked several times and then the night sky was back to normal. *Ch'ilsŏng* hung in his place, the Dipper forever keeping time. The Brilliant Pearls were merely pearls. The vision left me with a blinding headache, so violent I am only now recovering, many hours later. What am I to make of this vision, Grandmother? I know I should seek advice, but I am too ashamed to tell anyone. They will all think I am mad.

18th day of the 3rd moon,
17th year of King Chinp'yŏng

Grandmother, if I knew which square of paper inside you belonged to my madness of yesterday, I would retrieve it and destroy it. Please pay no mind to my starry rambling. I was still in the throes of my headache, and I'm sure I wrote much nonsense.

19th day of the 3rd moon, 17th year of King Chinp'yŏng

My sisters are helping Mother, so Lin Fang and I study alone. It is so strange, Grandmother. When I read Master Confucius on my own, I find many words of deep wisdom and kindness. Yet when Lord Lin Fang reads from the Master, his words are venomous and hard. Can two such opposite interpretations exist for the same set of words?

23rd day of the 3rd moon, 17th year of King Chinp'yŏng

I look out my window at night and recite the planets like I would chant a Buddhist mantra. From *Taeyang*, the sun, we have:

Susŏng (Mercury in the West), which means Star of Water
Kumsŏng (Venus in the West), which means Star of Metal
Hwasŏng (Mars in the West), which means Star of Fire
Moksŏng (Jupiter in the West), which means Star of Wood
Tosŏng (Saturn in the West), which means Star of Soil
Then, there is our Earth between *Kumsŏng* and *Hwasŏng*, which is shaped like a box, and our heavens that

astronomers say are round. Some of these planets are *um* and some are *yang.* There is an old legend that says if *Kumsŏng* (an *um,* feminine, planet) shines in the daytime, then a woman is destined to rule. Our city of gold, Kumsŏng, is named after this star of metal, and I hope one day a woman shall rule there, legend or no legend.

Will we ever know the truth about the stars? I am too young to venture a theory about our universe, I only know that I want to understand more deeply. I want to know all I can know. Why should it be forbidden?

25th day of the 3rd moon,
17th year of King Chinp'yŏng

Father's astronomers walked past my window this morning, but they did not look up to see me. They have been given instructions not to talk to me on pain of exile.

28th day of the 3rd moon, 17th year of King Chinp'yŏng

Though I am not allowed inside, Revered Ancestor, I know what is happening in the Silkworm Hall. The worms are spinning their cocoons. Fat and white. Everything that is valuable about them will soon be on the outside and they will no longer be necessary. They will be boiled and killed. Isn't that the way of all creators, Grandmother? Once they have given the world their great works, what need is left of them?

1st day of the 4th moon, 17th year of King Chinp'yŏng Ipha (Summer Begins)

Grandmother, it is the beginning of the fourth month, the time when farmers prepare their rice seedlings for transplant into the paddies, and all through the land, men and women are hoeing and weeding. I have served out my punishment and am free to move around the Fortress again. Father has decided to tour his lands before the onset of the great rains, and, perhaps to make amends for my captivity, has asked that I accompany him. We are to make the journey between Kumsŏng and the port of Pusan after the celebration of the Buddha's birthday, touring some of the province in between, and arrive home in time for the *Tano* festival.

7th day of the 4th moon, 17th year of King Chinp'yŏng

The silkworms have rested for eight days and now they are to be steamed. The worms die inside their cocoons, but they give up their thread to clothe our cold bodies and to adorn our palaces. Inside the Silkworm Hall, our servants are dipping the cocoons into hot water to loosen the strands and gently teasing them apart to be unwound onto spools. One filament from a single cocoon would stretch out of the palace gate and into the city, and it takes five such fibers to be twisted into a single thread.

8th day of the 4th moon, 17th year of King Chinp'yŏng

It is the Buddha's birthday today, and also my friend Chajang's.

You know, Grandmother, our tradition says that lighting a lantern on Buddha's birthday represents the purifying of the soul. Parents light one paper lantern for each child in their family to bring good luck, and here at Half-moon Fortress, we light hundreds of lamps so that the whole palace is ablaze with light.

The city is so beautiful with all the glowing lanterns. They are strung in trees and the citizens parade with them on long poles. After sunset, our family always climbs the mountain to view the spectacle of thousands of lanterns bobbing up the hills, like so many stars fallen to Earth. Last year, I lit a lantern and prayed for my own observatory. This year, I lit one and prayed to have no more starry visions. I cannot tell you how shaken I was to have my mother disappear before my very eyes.

9th day of the 4th moon,
17th year of King Chinp'yŏng
Kyerim, the Chicken Forest

Father and I began our journey by making offerings for good fortune at our ancestor shrine in Kyerim, the Chicken Forest. I love the story of our ancestor and this wooded land just outside the Half-moon Fortress. About five hundred years ago, King T'al-hae heard a rooster crow in this forest and went out to investigate. It was late at night and a strange mist hung over the trees. The king followed an eerie light coming from an old Chinese elm, and when he reached for it, found a golden box hanging from one of the tree's branches. Beneath the box sat a rooster, crying loudly. The old king opened the box and inside found a beautiful baby boy, whom he named Kim Al-chi after the Chinese character *kum* meaning "gold." King T'al-hae adopted Kim Al-chi and made him his heir, but our ancestor would not steal the proper place of the king's true-born son. One hundred eighty years later, when all the other heirs had died out, a descendent of Kim Al-chi became king, and we Kims have ruled ever since.

For many generations, our kingdom of Silla was called Kyerim, and our people are still sometimes called the Chicken People! I take it as a compliment, Grandmother.

10th day of the 4th moon,
17th year of King Chinp'yŏng
South of the Chicken Forest

Just south of the city, I saw something deeply troubling, Grandmother. The *ch'onmin*, or despised people — those without rank who perform taboo jobs like butchering meat — are allowed no access to the ground for burial. Instead they put their dead in a box, or a straw bag, or a jar, and hoist them to the tops of trees until they are nothing but bones. These bones they burn and scatter. We passed a village that had succumbed to an epidemic, and all the treetops bloomed with this awful fruit. Can rank be so important, Grandmother, that those without it are denied even a final resting place?

11th day of the 4th moon,
17th year of King Chinp'yŏng
Nam-san Mountain

We rested ourselves today at the fortress of Nam-san that Father commissioned several years ago and here will spend several days. Father solemnly told me the story that it was on this holy southern mountain, many, many years ago, that the six main chieftains of Silla gathered together and agreed to consolidate their land. They were about to choose a king, when they saw a great white horse fly into the sky leaving behind an egglike gourd. Inside the gourd was a boy called Pak Hyŏkkŏse, and the six chieftains crowned him the first king of Silla. As you know, this is a very holy place and there are many secret carvings of Buddha here.

12th day of the 4th moon, 17th year of King Chinp'yŏng

While Father met with his ministers, I took my ladies and rode out into the valleys. How poor little Moonbeam hates these treacherous mountain paths! Tigers are known to live among these passes, and we rode in fear of being pounced on from above.

I discovered many rough statues of Buddha the monks of the area have carved into the face of the mountain. Almost all are missing their noses because the old *mudang* break them off and grind them into tea. Superstitious women believe this will help them conceive children! Over the next hill, there exists a convent of Buddhist nuns, living humbly and chanting night and day. They wear humble clothes and shave their heads. As we made our way back to the fortress, their voices sped us along. I felt protected by their chants, Grandmother, and completely forgot to fear the tigers.

15th day of the 4th moon,
17th year of King Chinp'yŏng
Soman (Grain Fills)
Rice Villages

Today is *Soman,* Grandmother, the day when farmers transplant their rice from the seedbed to the fields. We rode south of Nam-san, past pale green rice paddies as far as the eye could see. The old men and woman were stooping in ankle-deep water and carefully loosening handfuls of seedlings. They carried them to a field that had been carefully prepared and pushed the young roots deep into the soft, wet soil. It appears to be such exhausting work, Grandmother, far worse than attending silkworms. All that stooping and pulling and careful replanting. If the rain is plentiful, it takes a peasant about twelve days to transplant even a small plot of rice. When I see them hard at work, it makes me a little ashamed of how much rice I leave in my bowl every meal.

16th day of the 4th moon,
17th year of King Chinp'yŏng
On the Road to Pusan

This morning I write to you on the finest paper in Silla. Ah! How my brush glides gracefully over it. As you know, Grandmother, our Silla paper is prized by the finest scholars in China. I am sure Lin Fang would love to get his hands on a roll of this.

I was presented this paper by the master of the factory we inspected yesterday. This is the same factory that supplies the decorative paper for the palace floors, sliding doors, windows, and lanterns. The buildings are set up on the shores of a rushing stream that turns a great waterwheel. The wheel then rotates a grindstone that pulverizes strips of mulberry bark into a fine wet mush. The workers then spread the mush over wire frames and allow it to dry and bleach in the sun. They buff it with stones until it is smooth and then remove it from the frame. Now I write to you upon it!

17th day of the 4th moon, 17th year of King Chinp'yŏng

There are many treacherous mountain passes as we travel in this direction and the way is very steep. Our servants ride ahead and set up our royal camp. Our tents are so luxurious with gold and silver and silken hangings that I feel as comfortable as in the palace.

Nothing seems to drive ill health away like new sights and experiences. Today a few of my ladies and I climbed a mountain and collected wild ginger. I made a tea of it and feel stronger than I have in many weeks. Not a single headache.

19th day of the 4th moon, 17th year of King Chinp'yŏng

Tonight, while I was outside gazing up at the waning moon, Father came and stood beside me. We have not spoken much on this journey, for he has been very busy talking to his subjects along the way and asking after their business.

"I know you think I am harsh with you," Father said,

"but sometimes you need to trust your elders." His voice was very soft, not at all like the stern ruler to whom I was becoming accustomed. "I learned the hard way to respect my elders' wishes."

"How so, Father?" I asked, for I could tell he was in the mood for talking.

"You know I came to the throne very young," he continued, "and it was many years before I took my responsibilities seriously. I loved to hunt, and I would hunt for days, completely ignoring the needs of the kingdom. My faithful defense minister, Kim Hu-jik, scolded me for this and reminded me that the Buddha forbids the killing of animals. Yet, I cared not what my old advisor had to say. I continued to hunt."

I had never heard my father speak of his early days as king, Grandmother, and this was very interesting to me.

"One day, worthy Kim Hu-jik died," Father said, "and he had asked to be buried at the crossroads I always passed on my way to the hunting fields. Soon I began to hear voices muttering each time I rode past that place, and it became clear to me the voices were coming from the grave of Kim Hu-jik.

"Even in death, he was still advising me. 'Take up your duties as king,' he said. 'Your people have need of you.'

Again and again I heard his voice and knew he would not rest until I minded his wisdom. To give Kim Hu-jik peace, I vowed to swear off hunting forever. It is a shame I heeded the old man in death as I never would in life."

I felt very sorry for Father just then, Grandmother. And ashamed of myself. I am young and I do not know everything. I vowed to be less rebellious on our return to Kumsŏng, and even to treat Lord Lin Fang with more respect — for Father's sake if for no other reason. Kim Hu-jik did not live to see Father become a powerful and honored king. He would have been very proud.

Father and I stood outside for a very long time until at last he cleared his throat and said it was time for bed.

20th day of the 4th moon,
17th year of King Chinp'yŏng
Harbor of Pusan

Today, we reached the sea, Grandmother! Our lazy river Naktong could never have prepared me for such a sight. We smelled the salt water long before we saw it, but when we crested the mountain, there it lay, like the slumbering blue-green Dragon King himself. We are spending a few days at Father's fortress here, the one with four gates that overlooks the harbor toward Yamato Japan. It is more rustic than Nam-san and Half-moon, but my room overlooks the crashing waves, and I am thrilled.

21st day of the 4th moon, 17th year of King Chinp'yŏng

We had barely settled in when word arrived of a Paekche army force harassing the Han River basin. One of Father's generals rode up to give us the bad news. We must head back immediately, Grandmother. No sooner had I said hello to the ocean, than I must bid it good-bye.

24th day of the 4th moon, 17th year of King Chinp'yŏng On the Road Home

Just a brief message tonight, Grandmother, for we have ridden hard all day, and I am exhausted. Our spies have penetrated the Paekche troops and send reports back of the enemies' numbers. Paekche has allied itself with Yamato Japan, and that is why Father wants to court our friends the Chinese. He hopes to use the Chinese to conquer all of ancient Chŏsŏn and unite the peninsula under Silla's rule. Of course, Paekche and Koguryŏ hope to do the same to us. We must all be careful. Hemmed in by more powerful neighbors, any one of the Three Kingdoms could be swallowed whole by outsiders.

I fear this escalation in the war with Paekche will give Lin Fang even more power at our court. Father will need his Chinese friends more than ever.

1st day of the 5th moon,
17th year of King Chinp'yŏng
Mangjong (Grain in Ear)
Half-moon Fortress, Kŭmsŏng

Everyone speaks of war, except those setting up for the *Tano* festival. The country people have come from far and wide to erect their booths and hawk their wares. The entire city vibrates with excitement.

5th day of the 5th moon, 17th year of King Chinp'yŏng

What an exciting, maddening, confusing *Tano*, Grandmother. The day was very warm, and threatened rain, but luckily none came to ruin the festivities. No matter what else happened, it was nice to spend a day without the thought of war.

We women began our morning by bathing in the mountain springs and washing our hair with iris water. The floral scent is so luxurious and pure, I love to breathe in the aroma while I lie on hot stones letting the sun slowly dry my hair. The married women cut the root of the flower to make hairpins, and we all — married and unmarried — rouged our cheeks to drive away evil spirits.

Down in the city, the tug-of-war game had already begun, and we quickly joined the women on the western team facing the men pulling from the east. Of course, only the unmarried men and women were allowed to compete, grasping the many branches of the thick hemp rope. This year, the ladies used their wits and weighed their *chima* with stones so that they would not be immediately dragged over. I tugged and tugged until I thought my arms would drop off, and when I finally surrendered my spot to another lady, the western team had a slight advantage. I'll rejoin the tug tomorrow. It usually goes on for three or more days.

After tug-of-war, we wandered through the courtyard, stopping at all the small vendors selling traditional mugwort cakes and beautifully colored cloth. My ladies and I watched the tightrope walkers and farm dancers, until we spied a large crowd and went over to investigate.

It was a *ssirŭm* match, Grandmother, and my ladies giggled with delight. The crowd parted at our appearance to allow us the best view, and to my surprise, I saw one of the contestants was Chajang!

I had not seen my friend since Father and I went on procession, and I thought I had succeeded in putting him from my mind completely. From what I could tell, he was definitely the favorite, thought he was pitted against a boy from the Sohn clan who is one of his rivals in the *hwarang*, and does everything almost as well as he. At the signal, they lunged for each other, each grappling and snatching at the other's loincloth to try to pull him over. The Sohn boy tried hard to topple Chajang out of the circle, and twice it looked like my friend would be defeated, but he managed to right himself before all was lost. At last, Chajang pulled his opponent over and the boy's hand touched the mat. A roar went up for Chajang! And the minister in charge presented him with the bull that was his prize as champion.

My little cousin, Chindŏk, ran up to meet me while the minister was bestowing the bull. I did not feel the pull of her hand, so mesmerized was I by Chajang. I had never seen him flushed from battle, and I felt my heart lurch. As he waved triumphantly to the crowd, his eyes fixed on mine for a long moment and I believe he became suddenly self-conscious. He rapidly turned away and shouted for his trousers.

"My waiting lady Mikiko from Yamato Japan says they have *ssirŭm* there, too. Only they call it *sumo* and the men are hugely fat!" Chindŏk informed me, pulling me away to swing with her. I lost Chajang in the crowd and gratefully turned my attention to the little girl.

Swinging is one of my favorite *Tano* activities and when Chindŏk and I stepped upon the wooden plank and pushed off, I was thrilled to be once more a creature of the air. When we were little children, Chajang and I would sometimes ride the same swing, screaming as we flew higher and higher. Now Chindŏk clung tightly to my waist and we soared over the crowds, taking in splashes of color and the branches of trees, laughing townspeople, and birds in their nests.

"Kick!" I cried to Chindŏk, and she threw out her little leg to hit a mulberry branch high up in the tree. She squealed with delight and shouted, "Again! Again!"

We swung until my little cousin was exhausted, and then I slowly eased up on the ropes until we came to a gentle standstill. I was sweating and my hair had escaped its braid. I was panting like a peasant woman in the field when Lord Lin Fang walked by.

"I suppose I should have expected such shameless behavior," he said, horrified by the way our women swing and sing and dance with men on this midsummer festival. "What will become of a kingdom when the heir to the throne behaves like this?" Perhaps it was my confused thoughts toward Chajang, and the unsettled way I felt while watching the *ssirŭm* match, but Lin Fang's words pierced my soul, Grandmother. I felt ashamed, as if I had done something wicked. I remembered the vow I made to Father and humbly bowed my head before my tutor.

"Forgive my immodesty, Lord Fang," I said, much to his surprise. "What would you have me do?"

"Go inside where you belong and do not come out until after dark. In China, our women are not allowed out onto the street until after nightfall, and then they must wear a veil. Stop making yourself an enticement and a distraction. That is what your father would want, Lady Sŏndŏk."

My own guilty conscience compelled me to obey,

Grandmother. So here I sit, watching the festivities from the window, my ladies-in-waiting dismayed at having to miss out on all the games and masque dramas and other festivities.

Is Chajang out there looking for me? Why do I even ask this question? It can lead to nothing but heartbreak.

9th day of the 5th moon, 17th year of King Chinp'yŏng

The *hwarang* are preparing to face the armies of Paekche. They are boisterous and excited, racing about on their horses, and hunting for sport to hone their archery skills. I caught only a glimpse of Chajang, riding out with the rest, but his face was set and somber. Not full of fire like the other boys.

15th day of the 5th moon, 17th year of King Chinp'yŏng Haji (Summer Solstice)

Since today was *Haji,* the longest day of the year, I took the opportunity to climb the mountain to Hwangyŏng

Monastery to give homage to the Three Spirits: *Sanshin, Toksŏng,* and *Ch'ilsŏng.* Pardon me if I am wrong, Grandmother, but as I've heard the story, Great-grandfather Chin-hung originally intended to build a palace on that land. However, when they were digging the foundation, the workmen spied a dragon lurking about the construction site. Great-grandfather Chin-hung wisely decided to build a monastery instead, and named it after the Imperial Dragon.

I feel awe every time I approach the enormous main hall with its three gigantic golden Buddha statues in front. I feel them encouraging me along the path to Enlightenment. And I need much encouragement these days.

I offered fresh fruit and incense at the alter of the Three Spirits and then, leaving my waiting women behind, climbed to a niche in the mountain where there was a rough-hewn Buddha tucked away in a cave. I have always felt closer to this Buddha than to the rich ones of gold. He seems ancient to me and more powerful.

As I approached the shrine, I thought I heard the sound of weeping carried on noisy insect wings. It was true. A young man sat before the Buddha with his head in his hands. It was Chajang, Grandmother! He jumped when he saw me and wiped his eyes roughly.

"Lady Sŏndŏk, I did not know you were here," he said stiffly.

"Chajang, we are old friends," I chided him, though my mouth felt suddenly dry. "You do not need to be so formal. What is bothering you?"

He hesitated, but after some prodding finally admitted his despair. He had been hunting yesterday with the other *hwarang* and had wounded a pheasant. When he followed her back to her nest, he found her crying over her poor helpless chicks, who would certainly die without her. His shame and remorse was too great to bear, and he ran here, to beg the forgiveness of the Buddha.

"Little Weaving Maid," he said, using my old nickname. "I have broken one of the five rules of the *hwarang*. I have killed indiscriminately. I have been hunting many times, and killed many things before without thinking. But this time I saw the horror of it. The Buddha says we should eat only vegetables and grain, and harm no living animal. If I cannot justify hunting, how am I to justify war?"

I tried to comfort him, Grandmother. I even reached out and gently patted his back. But nothing would console him. I finally left him and walked slowly back to the Half-moon Fortress. I am worried about Chajang going into battle. He is no warrior. How is he to serve his king by killing our enemies of Paekche Kingdom if he is this upset over killing a bird?

18th day of the 5th moon, 17th year of King Chinp'yŏng

I have passed Chajang twice in the courtyard, but each time he has appeared deep in thought. I am worried for my friend, Grandmother. And I am angry at myself for letting my fears for him disturb my studies.

19th day of the 5th moon, 17th year of King Chinp'yŏng

It has become so hot, we have all switched to our lightweight hempen *chima*. Even these are soon limp with perspiration. My hair is plastered to the back of my neck and I feel like a wilted flower. It has not rained in weeks, Grandmother, and there appears to be no relief in sight. I feel especially sorry for the *hwarang* who must practice fighting in this weather. They are all red in the face and half collapsed with exhaustion after their training sessions. I started to take Chajang some iced persimmon water out of pity, but then thought better of it. I do not know if it would be welcome.

20th day of the 5th moon, 17th year of King Chinp'yŏng

It is so very hot, Grandmother, and everyone is in a foul mood. Food is scarce in the countryside. Little is ripe yet, but the supplies from last autumn are nearly used up. People fight in the marketplace for what little there is, and rage at the merchants who charge exorbitant prices. While we have enough to eat inside Half-moon Fortress, the air here is full of black, biting flies and whining mosquitoes. I have two waiting women fanning me even as I write this. If only it would rain. At least there would be some relief.

25th day of the 5th moon, 17th year of King Chinp'yŏng

When all is quiet at night, I can hear music coming from the rice fields beyond Kumsŏng. The peasants are playing upon pipes and beating their drums to drive away hunger.

They must do something to cheer themselves during this exhausting planting season. Their music is frenzied and wild, like something older than time itself.

28th day of the 5th moon, 17th year of King Chinp'yŏng

It was so hot inside the hall, even with my ladies fanning me, that I stole away. I can no longer study my star charts openly. Many of my waiting women would be only too happy to report me to Father and earn rewards for themselves. Nor may I speak with the court astronomers. They are forbidden still to converse with me.

I made my way to the Royal Ice House, which is a cave cut out of the hillside that has been reinforced with a brick archway. The blocks of ice our servants cut last winter are slowly melting inside, where they have been stacked in layers of hay and sawdust. I settled down between two puddles that were made as the blue ice dripped through its cloak of hay, and unrolled two separate natal charts — mine and Chajang's. Was it wrong to look for a sign among the stars, Grandmother? To see if Chajang and I were destined to be together? Could I find some conjunction in our future, or were we destined to be like the cosmic Herdboy and Weaving Maid, separated forever by the milky Celestial River?

I was so lost in my thoughts, I did not hear his footsteps approach. When I looked up, Chajang was standing before me. As if I had conjured him from the stars on my scroll.

"I thought you were forbidden from stargazing," Chajang said, as I guiltily rolled up my charts.

"I am," I replied. "But I cannot seem to help myself."

"That which is forbidden has a powerful draw, does it not?"

"We cannot change our natures," I replied, and my face felt hot.

Chajang looked sadly away. "No, I do not suppose we can."

I stood up and sidled around him. "I was just going. You may have your turn in the cool air."

"No, do not let me disturb you," Chajang said. "I come here to think, but I believe I have thought more than is healthy these past few weeks."

Chajang turned and walked away absently, as if he did not know where he was or what he had been doing. I watched his strong, straight back, and then I lay down, turning my eyes to the dripping ice above, Grandmother. I lay there a very long time, while the ice melted like an echo of winter upon my hot, cracked lips.

1st day of the 6th moon,
17th year of King Chinp'yŏng
Sŏso (Little Heat)

We call today *Sŏso,* or the Little Heat, though I don't know why, because it is murderously hot and the air has become soupy and close. Why on Earth did I ever pray for rain, Grandmother? The monsoons have burst upon us and washed out the roads, turning everything to thick red mud. Out in the countryside, torrents of water flood the rice paddies and tiny fish swim through the channels. There is little to do in the palace but sit inside and watch the water fall in curtains from the eaves. Lin Fang says we must use this opportunity for intensive study, but when I try to write, the paper puckers from the humidity and the ink pools unattractively.

My sisters and I play chess to pass the time when not studying, but it is little fun for me because they can never beat me. I am always the first to cross the river and pick off their counselors and take their king. I need a more challenging partner.

2nd day of the 6th moon,
17th year of King Chinp'yŏng

I am sticky and wet and miserable. The rain has done nothing to dispel the heat. It has only turned to steam.

15th day of the 6th moon,
17th year of King Chinp'yŏng
Taeso (Big Heat)

Grandmother, forgive me, for I have been very neglectful of you. I have not changed your rice in many days, nor have I offered any prayers. I feel you are angry with me, which is why I have this awful headache.

There was a brief break in the rain today and Chajang came to see if I might ride out with him. It was the first time I had seen him since the day in the ice house, and he seemed to have something important to discuss. As my lessons were over for the day, I saw no reason why I should not go.

He mounted his horse and I mounted Moonbeam, and we rode out into the countryside, following the South Stream. Overhead, the sky boiled with gray-green clouds, which hung so low I felt I could touch them. We stopped at a lush green field that glowed with red-purple hibiscus. At the water's edge, old peasant women were beating their laundry with two small bats, one for each hand — softening the fabric and smoothing out the wrinkles. That rhythmic beating is one of my favorite sounds.

"Your father has asked me to take a position at court instead of going off to war," said Chajang at last. The last time we spoke, his voice had been hollow and far away. But today, the old mellowness was back. It seemed to have deepened in just a few weeks, and there were other changes, too. His jaw was stronger. His cheek a little downier. His eyes more serious.

"That is a great honor," I replied, thinking, *Praise the heavens. He will not be killed in the battle with Paekche.* "The king loved your father and you have always proven yourself wise beyond your years."

Chajang looked at me, and my heart nearly stopped beating. There was something so pure and passionate in his gaze. He took my hand and spoke slowly.

"There is something you need to know, Weaving Maid. Something I have been afraid to tell you."

"What, dear friend?" I asked.

"I have decided to enter the monastery at Hwangyŏng," he said, and my heart began to beat again, but so sadly, Grandmother. So sadly.

"The horror I felt over killing that pheasant proved to me that I cannot become a warrior," he continued, though it was difficult for me to comprehend what he was saying. "Nor do I desire to serve at court. I have decided to devote my life to the understanding of a higher truth. I want to become a monk."

"You are barely fourteen years old," I said, trying to reason with him. "Can you really know your own heart so well?"

"There was a time, when we were children, I dared to think —" He looked at me with pain in his eyes, then looked away. "But you are Holy Bone and I am True Bone, and it was forbidden to us. Gradually, the Buddha crowded out all earthly attachments, and now I know my fate. I feel it as strongly as you feel you are to be queen."

I wanted so badly to throw myself upon him and beg him to reconsider, Grandmother, but what was I to do? My friend was right. All my dreams of him were but weak, girlish fantasies. I am to be queen of Silla. Like him, I can afford only one passion.

"When you are queen and I am a great monk, we will do many important things together, my noble Weaving Maid," said Chajang. I was quiet.

"But I need your help," he said at last. "Your father was furious when I told him my decision. I have never seen him so angry. Will you speak on my behalf, Sŏndŏk? Will you make him understand?"

I told him I would try, and then we sat for some time in silence, listening to the beating of the laundry bats.

I am sorry. Grandmother. My headache is too severe. I can write no more tonight.

16th day of the 6th moon, 17th year of King Chinp'yŏng

Desires are our downfall. Desires are our downfall. We cannot cling to earthly passions, says the Buddha, for they will always disappoint us.

20th day of the 6th moon, 17th year of King Chinp'yŏng

I overheard Lin Fang speaking to Father today and I think they were talking of Chajang. "You must make an example of him," Lin Fang was saying. "How are you to control your subjects if you cannot even control a young boy?" I hurried away from the courtyard, Grandmother. Where are Father's other courtiers? It seems he listens to no one anymore but that Chinese ambassador.

Oh, Grandmother, the very worst has happened. Father has ordered Chajang put to death!

First he tried flattery to convince my friend. "You have a bright future, my boy, why won't you take up the position you were born to?" But Chajang refused. Next, father pleaded. "Won't you help an old king who needs good men?" But Chajang refused. At last, Father commanded in front of the entire *hwabaek*, "You will take the position I have assigned you, and we will hear no more about this monk business," Father practically screamed. And I could see Lin Fang behind him, smirking. "If you will not bend to my will, I will have you executed."

And Chajang replied, "I would rather die keeping the laws of Buddha for one day than live for one hundred years breaking them."

This is all Lin Fang's fault! Chajang is now in prison, and I am off to plead with Father. Grandmother, I beg of you, soften my father's heart!

I am back from Father's chambers, and more exhausted than I can ever remember being, Grandmother.

I found him staring out the window, while Mother tried to make him eat. The small table was covered with all his favorite foods, but he angrily waved her away. With a sigh, Mother removed the table with its cold rice and untouched delicacies and slipped behind the paper door. She shook her head at me as if to say, "There is no use."

"Father," I said, kneeling beside him. "Allow me leave to speak to you."

He looked over with a very unpleasant expression, as if steeling himself against me.

"Confucius said, 'To execute a man without having admonished, that is called cruelty,'" I reminded him.

"Do not use Confucius against me," growled Father. "I warned Chajang. I gave him every chance to please his king. I cannot have my subjects willfully disobeying me."

I observed him for a long moment, trying to decide which was the best way to touch his heart. The only sound was the hard rain upon the roof. At last I spoke.

"I am only going to tell you a story," I said. "One you might recognize."

Father turned back to the window, staring over the flooded courtyard. Fallen leaves of the gingko trees had made a slick, yellow carpet.

"There was once a lonely couple who prayed for a son," I began. "Every day they went to the shrine of the god *Ch'ilsŏng*, the Great Northern Dipper, who looks after childbirth. They offered rice and bolts of silk. They lit incense and bowed low before the shrines. The mother wept because she was childless. The father cursed his fate. One night, this man went to the shrine and made a vow that if the god should grant him a son, he would make that boy a bridge to eternal paradise. That same night, the man's wife lay dreaming. She dreamed a falling star fell from heaven and entered her womb. Nine months later, she was brought to bed of a son on the Buddha's birthday."

Father hung his head. He knew this story very well. It was one they told about Chajang.

"Father, he is not disobeying you. He is obeying the will of Heaven."

"Sŏndŏk," Father said wearily, after a long silence. "I am not a cruel man. I wanted Chajang to take a position at court partly for your sake."

I was startled, Grandmother. Why for my sake?

"The Holy Bone line is dying out. I have fathered only daughters," he said. "The only other Holy Bone is your cousin, Chindŏk, also female. Chajang is of noble birth. He is True Bone. I thought one day you might marry."

Grandmother, I cannot tell you how shocked I was by my father's words. We of the Holy Bone have only ever married our cousins, so that we might keep the lineage pure. To marry with a True Bone was unthinkable. And yet Father considered it for my sake.

"Father," I said, "thank you for thinking of my happiness, but Chajang will never be my husband. He belongs to the Buddha. We must both accept that."

Father nodded very slowly, then asked to be left alone to pray. Grandmother, please touch the heart of your son and show him the right path. As followers of Buddha, we are forbidden to kill even an animal. Please, Grandmother, for his own soul's sake — do not let Father make a dire mistake.

27th day of the 6th moon,
17th year of King Chinp'yŏng

Will it never stop raining?

1st day of the 7th moon,
17th year of King Chinp'yŏng
Ipchu'u (Autumn Begins)

We have had no word from Father all day. No one knows what he is thinking. How blissful those hot, fly-filled days of several weeks ago seem now. Little did I know how much worse it could get.

I could not sleep, Grandmother, and so I have brought papers and ink and a lantern to the spot behind Half-moon Fortress where I record my observations.

The people down below in the city know that Chajang is in danger. His family was very popular among the people, and they are singing for his release. I understand friends of Chajang have sponsored a *kut* with the old *mudang*, in hopes of saving his life.

The city of Kumsŏng looks so beautiful under the stars, Grandmother. The torches burn like molten gold and reflect off the black-tiled roofs. The hill tombs of my ancestors swell up under the streets like man-made mountains. The city waits, like the rest of us, to hear the fate of Chajang.

4th day of the 7th moon, 17th year of King Chinp'yŏng

I have been thinking a great deal about what has bothered my friend. How are we to wage war against our enemies when our Buddha forbids us to kill? When I am queen, how am I to protect these citizens down below without breaking the laws of Heaven? Like his father before him, Grandfather was obviously troubled by this question. He left the throne to become a monk, and you, Grandmother, shaved your head and followed him, becoming a Buddhist nun. Are these the only two choices? Murder or the monastery?

6th day of the 7th moon, 17th year of King Chinp'yŏng

Father met with his ministers all day, but I have no idea what was said. No one has told me anything. Everyone is speaking in whispers and always there is Lin Fang. I feel so responsible for this calamity, Grandmother. Had Father only had a son, he would not be breaking taboos to marry me outside of the Holy Bone. He would not have put pressure on Chajang to take a position at court for my sake, and my friend would not have had to defy him. All this misery, and still more to come, because I was born a girl. I have come to a decision, Grandmother. If the gods spare Chajang, I will put away my stargazing instruments forever. I will give up my astronomy and become a dutiful daughter in the Confucian way. I will offer only prayers for a brother, and set forth no more of my selfish ramblings.

I beseech you, Grandmother, to intervene.

7th day of the 7th moon, 17th year of King Chinp'yŏng

I do not write for you tonight, Grandmother. Tonight I write for Chajang. If I could speak to him one last time, this is the story I would tell:

They say on *Ch'ilsŏk*, the seventh day of the seventh month, no magpies or crows are seen on Earth because they have all flown up to Heaven to make a bridge for the Herdboy and the Weaving Maid. A long time ago, back when the tiger smoked his pipe, there lived a princess who was more accomplished at silk weaving than any girl in the kingdom. She wove such lifelike trees that birds came and nested in them, such refreshing streams that fish leaped from the river to try to swim upstream. One day, her father, the king, saw she had woven the face of a handsome young man into her tapestry and knew that it was time she was married. He took counsel of his ministers and together they decided on a prince of the neighboring kingdom who was renowned for his cattle herds. No one attended his livestock more tenderly or diligently. The king thought the two talented youths would make a perfect match.

The day came when they were married, and sure enough, as the king predicted, the two fell desperately in love. They spent every waking hour together, composing poetry and staring deeply into one another's eyes. So greatly did they love one another, that the Weaving Maid forgot all about her silk and the Herdboy so neglected his cattle that they began to waste away and die. "This will never do!" roared the king, and he ordered the young lovers separated, and allowed them to see each other for only one night in the year.

As you know, dear friend, these two poor souls have become the stars *Kyŏnu* and *Chingnyŏ*, and they are brightest on the seventh day of the seventh month, each shining on opposite sides of the great Celestial River. All the magpies and crows of Earth take pity on the lovers this night and make a bridge across the River so that *Kyŏnu* and

Chingnyŏ might embrace. As it so happens, rain almost always falls on this night, which we say is the lovers' tears at having to part once more. Rain is falling now, as it fell just an hour ago, when I stood on one side of the Moon Spirit Bridge and watched you released on the other side of the river. Father agreed to pardon you on the condition you left the palace immediately and went to live with the monks at Hwangyŏng. We had no opportunity to speak, but merely gazed at one another through the gentle rain as you were led off.

No magpies came for us tonight, dear friend. But as you bowed to me, I had another one of my visions. The stars wheeled in the heavens and took the shape of you and I standing in the courtyard of Hwangyŏng Monastery. We were both as old as Father is now and we were gazing up at a nine-story Buddhist pagoda, higher and more splendid than any building in Silla. We were smiling at one another, knowing we had built this wonder together but that it would always stand between us — you in your world, and me in mine. Then the vision was gone.

And when I looked back, so were you.

I have gathered together my armillary spheres and incense clocks, my sundials and star charts, and I have
packed them in a lacquered box. This box I have buried in
the spot behind the palace where I always sat to make my
calculations, the spot I deem best for viewing the heavens.
I had dreamed of one day building an observatory on this
place, a tower to take me halfway to the stars. I would have
had the base be square to represent the Earth and the
tower round, as the heavens are round. I would have used
the Great Dipper *Ch'ilsŏng* as my guide and laid out the
tower so that on the equinoxes the sun lit up the whole
floor, and on the solstices the sun left all black. It would
have been a testament to Silla's astronomical glory and I
would have gone there every night to construct my own
charts and learn to rule my kingdom wisely.

But I have made a bargain, Grandmother. You have
kept your part, and now I shall keep mine. Chajang has
been spared. I bid good-bye to chart and sphere and
dreams of towers. From this day forward, I am a dutiful
Confucian daughter.

9th day of the 7th moon, 17th year of King Chinp'yŏng

Grandmother, this is Sŏndŏk. I offer you fresh rice and beg you grant my father a son.

10th day of the 7th moon, 17th year of King Chinp'yŏng

Lord Lin Fang says I have become a very diligent pupil. I honor him, Grandmother, for putting up with my foolishness as long as he did. Lord Lin Fang is a very wise man.

11th day of the 7th moon, 17th year of King Chinp'yŏng

Today, I practiced my courtly dancing and played upon my *kayagum* as refined ladies of the court should do. I made offerings to our ancestors that they might grant my father a son.

15th day of the 7th moon,
17th year of King Chinp'yŏng
Ch'oso (End of Heat) Baekjung Festival

It is said that the Heavenly Official passes judgment on a person's virtue three times in a year: on the fifteenth day of the first month, on the fifteenth day of the tenth month, and today, on *Baekjung.* My virtue has been lacking up until this point, Grandmother, but no longer. I am changed.

The yearly weaving contest that ends on Hangawi, begins today. It is still customary for each princess to lead a team of women in order to set a good example for the common people. Sŏnwha, Ch'ŏn-myong, and I each have our faction of court ladies, and we are twisting hempen thread to weave on the festival of Hangawi. The losing parties must treat the winner. I feel honored to engage in such meaningful woman's work, Grandmother.

18th day of the 7th moon,
17th year of King Chinp'yŏng

Once more, Grandmother, I beg you to use your influence among our ancestral spirits and present Father with a son.

20th day of the 7th moon,
17th year of King Chinp'yŏng

Father spends much time closeted with Lin Fang. I hope that Father heeds the counsel of his wisest advisor. Forgive any unkind words I used against my tutor, Grandmother. He is the best of men and suffers me admirably.

23rd day of the 7th moon,
17th year of King Chinp'yŏng

Sŏndŏk brings you peace, Grandmother. And touching my head to the floor, I beg you help my father conceive a son.

24th day of the 7th moon,
17th year of King Chinp'yŏng

I have twisted much hempen fiber, Grandmother. Usually young women pray to the stars for help with their weaving skills, but I pray to you, instead. When I walk out at night, I keep my eyes on the ground.

Grandmother, what have I done?

My prayers have found their mark, but not in the way I intended! I was willing to give up my place as my father's heir and my hopes of being Silla's first queen, but they cannot do this to Mother! You must stop them. Grandmother, please!

The monastery has swallowed everyone I love!

I can practice this Confucian charade no longer! It has become all too clear what Lin Fang has been discussing with my father this past month. In the hopes of producing an heir, he has convinced Father to set Mother aside.

Paekche made another attempt on the Han River basin, and that was all Lin Fang and his faction at court needed. "Your enemies do not respect you because you have produced no son," Lin Fang said. "Even your own subjects dare to defy you." Without a new wife, the king cannot father a legitimate son, and without a son, the kingdom will fall to ruins. Lin Fang has convinced Father that his ancestors are angry that he has produced no male issue to honor them. They are working through his enemies in Paekche and through Chajang to undermine his authority. They are even sending an eclipse on the first day of the tenth month. Can he doubt their displeasure?

Father has not banished Mother, but what choice does she have but to enter the monastery? Should she stay at the palace and watch another, younger woman take her place? Should she be expected to wait upon the new queen — to brush her hair and serve her meals? What choice does she have but to become a Buddhist nun and hide herself from the world?

Grandmother!

27th day of the 7th moon, 17th year of King Chinp'yŏng

We do what we can to comfort Mother. I took her a dish of chestnuts and water sweetened with dried persimmons, but she stared at her favorite meal with as much appetite as if I had offered her acorns and a goblet of seawater. I moved the tray and sat beside her on her silk mat, where she dutifully embroidered one of Father's robes. While my chamber is stacked high with books, splotched with over-turned ink pots, and dusty from shedding horsehair writing brushes, Mother's chamber is pure and bright. She designed her own floor paper in green and blue like interlocking waves, and has her servants varnish it so it does not tear.

Nothing in Mother's life has prepared her for this sort of betrayal. She has always spent her days dutifully tending the silkworms, weaving, and overseeing the kitchen and storehouses. She has been an exemplary wife in all ways but one. It is so unfair, Grandmother.

Sŏnwha pulled me aside.

"This morning, I heard a *mudang* singing a song of Mother's exile," my sister said, weeping. I thought then of the old *mudang* who had cast our fortunes on New Year's Day, and what she predicted for Mother. Traveler Thinks of Home. At the time I had no idea what that could mean, but now, it was all too clear.

"Father will change his mind," I said, trying to cheer her, though I was as upset as she. Sŏnwha, Ch'ŏn-myong, and I became hoarse from crying, our eyes red, and our braids undone. Mother, on the other hand, sat and sewed with an untroubled brow.

"I have only myself to blame," sighed Mother. "I could not give him a son."

"It is not your fault," Ch'ŏn-myong cried. "The gods did not will it."

"Girls, please do not despair," said she. "I am past childbearing age. Your father is only doing this for the good of his kingdom, not out of hatred for me. Or for you, dear Sŏndŏk."

As if I cared about myself, Grandmother.

Later

Down below, outside the gate, I hear an old woman singing as she passes by. She wails Mother's favorite song — the long, sad ballad of the Dragon King of the Sea coming for an innocent princess. The girl pleads with her father not to let her be taken away, but her father, the king, is distracted by a string of fire pearls that bubble up from the Yellow Sea. Rescue her, the old woman sings. Do not let your daughter be taken from her home. But the old king does not hear, and as the Great Northern Dipper rises, the song grows fainter until it finally fades away. I do not know whom I hate more, Grandmother. Lin Fang for wishing my mother set aside, or the old *mudang* who sings as if Heaven had already ordained it so.

28th day of the 7th moon, 17th year of King Chinp'yŏng

I have just returned from Hwangyŏng where I went to pray for Mother. I had hoped to speak with Chajang, my only friend, but I was told he is off praying in the mountains. This will be my mother's life, before long. No more tending silkworms or overseeing festivals. No more colorful silk *chima* or jewelry or lovingly carved hairpins. Nothing but rough hemp and a shaved head for our most beautiful queen.

Oh, how I wish I could take back all the unkind thoughts I've had about her. All the cruel words I have used. I have tried to speak with Father, but he refuses to see me, knowing, perhaps, I could change his mind. Grandmother, I feel so helpless. There must be something I can do.

1st day of the 8th moon, 17th year of King Chinp'yŏng Paengno (White Dews)

The Buddha takes what I love. Confucius says we must obey the will of the father. I can think of only one other place to turn for help. Forgive me, Grandmother. I cannot give up without trying one last resort.

2nd day of the 8th moon, 17th year of King Chinp'yŏng

It is nearly dawn, and I have just returned from the house of the old *mudang* who read our fortunes on New Year's Day. I wore old, borrowed clothes so that no one would recognize me, and bribed one of my women to slip me out of the gate. My heart was in my throat the entire time, but no one recognized me.

It was a long walk from the Moon Spirit Bridge into her part of the city. Torches flared against the darkness, throwing shadows on the wooden houses with their black-tiled roofs and stone fences. The old *mudang* lived on a backstreet in the heart of the city. It was a very small building with a thatched roof, and one she shared with her large family. When her children learned my identity, they dropped to the ground in terror. Not her, though. She almost seemed to be expecting me.

There was little furniture inside the *mudang*'s house, just a few mats and an altar set up to the god of the Great Northern Dipper, *Ch'ilsŏng.* He was represented as a stern-looking man wearing a halo of seven stars. Bowls of rice and plates of fruit were set up before his portrait and several candles burned. Overhead, the old *mudang* had stretched a grid of string between the roof beams and pasted paper onto it to form a ceiling. I heard rats scampering across the paper above.

"I have come about my mother," I said roughly, for I was nervous and unused to being treated with so little ceremony.

"Your father is setting her aside," the *mudang* said, more of a statement than a question.

"I wish to sponsor a *kut* for her," I replied. "To pacify our ancestors." I was more afraid than I have ever been, Grandmother. More afraid of this fearsome, crazy-looking old woman than I had ever been of Lin Fang. She squinted at me and frowned.

"Your ancestors respected the *mudang*," she said. "Some were even shaman priests themselves, ensuring the good fortune and health of the nation. The court has strayed too far into a foreign faith. You are forgetting the old ways."

"The old ways are superstitious," I said. "We have no use for them anymore. Before we found the Way of the Buddha, servants used to be buried alive with their masters when the master died. Do you think that was good?"

"I see that in a time of true crisis you have sought me out." She turned her back to me. "Why not pray at Hwangyŏng?"

"I tried that," I nearly shouted. "Now I will try anything!"

The old women's children peered at me from the ground where they were still crouched in their bows. They waited fearfully for their mother to reply.

"There is good and bad in every faith, Princess Sŏndŏk," she said at last. "When you reject the old ways, you reject your ancestors. You become a tree without roots. You must water your roots even as you branch out from above. You must find a balance."

I did not care to be lectured. "Will you help me?" I demanded.

"I will hold a *kut* for the queen," the old woman replied wearily. "But it is probably already too late. You should look to yourself, Princess Sŏndŏk. Your personal spirit god is displeased you have forsaken him."

I ignored her last remark and set a date and place for the *kut*. I promised her bags of rice and bolts of precious silk. Now back in my room at the palace, I am amazed at what I've done.

I know the first kings of Silla were shaman priests, Grandmother. For generations, our kings and queens relied on the *mudang*. Yet you and Grandfather, like Grandfather's parents, King Pob-hung and Queen P'o-do, ended your days in a Buddhist monastery. Tell me, Grandmother — just which ancestors am I supposed to please?

3rd day of the 8th moon, 17th year of King Chinp'yŏng

I have confided my meeting with the *mudang* to no one. Not even the serving woman who helped me slip away knows where I went. I am sure she believes I was out to meet an admirer.

Mother is giving away her beautiful clothes in preparation for entering the monastery.

Oh, how I wish I could talk to Chajang.

4th day of the 8th moon, 17th year of King Chinp'yŏng

Traditionally, Silla's queens have come from the Pak clan, but that is now out of the question. Lin Fang urges Father to look to the Sohn clan, and in particular to a girl named Seung-man. She is barely older than I am, Grandmother! The *mudang*'s *kut* must work.

5th day of the 8th moon,
17th year of King Chinp'yŏng

In the middle of all this, we princesses are to pretend that nothing is wrong. That our mother is not about to be taken from us. That our father is not about marry a girl young enough to be our sister. We are to twist hempen thread for the weaving contest on Hangawi, ten days away. My fingers work mechanically, but my mind is many leagues away from here.

8th day of the 8th moon,
17th year of King Chinp'yŏng

Tonight is the *kut*, Grandmother. I had to tell my sisters, for their presence is required, and I also have asked a few of Mother's waiting women to attend. We have been given leave to travel to Mother's family house under the pretext of her saying good-bye to her older brother and sister-in-law, and there the *mudang* will meet us. Mother's family knows and understands the importance of this ritual, and they have their own reasons for assisting. They have no desire to see the Sohn clan gain ascendancy over them.

I am afraid of the ghosts the *mudang* will call up

tonight, Grandmother. They say the dead are toxic to the living, even when they mean well. I have heard countless stories of dead grandmothers reaching out to fondly stroke the cheek of a new infant, only to have her touch cause it to wither and die. Perhaps the *mudang* will call you forth tonight. Perhaps you will not be happy to attend.

11th day of the 8th moon, 17th year of King Chinp'yŏng

After three frightening days, the *kut* is at long last over. I am so exhausted I can barely lift my hand. I will write more tomorrow.

12th day of the 8th moon, 17th year of King Chinp'yŏng

My sleep last night was tortured and full of fitful dreams. I cannot tell you with certainty, Grandmother, what was real and what came to me in slumber. The two seem almost interchangeable, as if I have spent the last four days in a trance.

I will start at the beginning.

When Mother first saw the *mudang* waiting at her ancestral house, she was not pleased. She had accepted her fate, she said, and we must, too. But her brother and sister-in-law pleaded with her. Ch'ŏn-myong, Sŏnwha, and I begged, and for the good of the family she was leaving behind, Mother agreed to the *kut*.

The *mudang* had already set up her altar to the god Ch'ilsŏng, and her assistants were laying out food and drink to offer the many gods. As I learned, the *kut* is too much for any one woman to perform, and at various times through the three days, her assistants took over a role.

The *kut* started with the *mudang* purifying the space. She beat upon a traditional *changgo* drum, which is shaped like a larger jar pinched in the middle, while one assistant shook a brass rattle, and a third played on pipes. She chewed big mouthfuls of white rice, and then, spinning, violently spat it out to the four corners of the yard. She made offerings to the gods that govern different parts of the house: to *Sŏngju*, the house site god, who lives in the roof beam above the porch, and to *Tŏju*, who lives in a small bottle tucked between the soy sauce pots in the backyard. She sang long songs about the origins of these gods and how they protected us. Then she moved inside and made an offering to Samsin Halmŏni, the birth grandmother goddess, who lives in the inner room. When she laid a bowl of fresh white rice before the Samsin Halmŏni, I thought of you, Grandmother, and prayed you would not find displeasure at this ritual.

After the house had been purified, the *mudang* ordered a rice pot of water placed on the hearth and threw in a handful of herbs. On top of the water, she set a porcelain bowl to catch wood imps and other mischievous spirits that might plague us. The imps would be attracted to the herbs and when the water boiled away, they would be trapped under the bowl.

Next came a long and frightening chant to call the other bad influences out of the house. The *mudang* and her assistants stood in the courtyard playing upon the pipes and drum. The old woman chanted to the spirits of the *yŏngsan,* the ghosts of those who had died unmarried, or without children, or violently, or far from home. Her voice was beautiful and strong, yet the words of her chant chilled me to the core.

Yŏngsan of those whose heads were struck off
Yŏngsan of those who were butchered by Paekche
Yŏngsan of those who were impaled by Koguryŏ
Yŏngsan of those who died in childbirth

On and on she sang and each death was more grisly and frightening than the last. She gestured to my aunt and uncle to bring the food they had prepared out into the courtyard. Because *yŏngsan* have no descendants to prepare ritual feasts for them, they are always hungry, and always looking to do harm. The old woman hurled a haunch of pork over the wall, out into the fields so that the *yŏngsan* might chase it. Then she gestured for us to finish the food. We fell on it hungrily, Grandmother, for the *kut* had already been going on for six or more hours.

The house was now safe for us to enter, and we rested for a while inside. When the *mudang* had recovered her strength, the *kut* continued. She began this portion by ridding Mother of the Red Disaster, a cloud of misfortune that hangs over some people and brings calamity upon them. For this, she took two sharp swords (the same I had seen her walk upon during Slaves' Day months ago), and began violently chopping the air around Mother's head. I feared Mother's skull would be struck clean from her neck, but the *mudang* was skilled and Mother was safe.

Next, the old woman changed her garments and began to call upon the *Kamang*, who are our ancestral gods. She called upon Kim Al-chi, the founder of our dynasty, and on Pak Hyŏkkŏse, the founder of Mother's people. First, she sang songs praising them and their deeds, then she invited them to descend upon her and give our mother advice. She donned different *chima* for each ancestor and her voice changed accordingly. Through the *mudang,* our ancestors told us we had offended in this way and that way. We were never dutiful enough. They demanded gifts of rice and cloth and wine before they would leave. The angry voices of our ancestors were deeply troubling to me, and my sisters hid behind Mother the entire time. This portion of the *kut* lasted for hours and hours.

At different times, our exhaustions would overcome us and we would all fall asleep. Then, just as we began to dream, the *mudang's* drum would wake us again. Once when I woke, she was singing the long, infinitely sad tale of Princess Pari, the patroness of all shaman priestesses. Princess Pari was the seventh daughter of the king, whose birth so displeased her father that he had her locked in a jeweled box with a jar of milk and cast adrift at sea. But Pari did not die. Golden turtles supported the chest and took it to an old fisherman couple, who raised her. Pari lived a happy life until the day the king and queen fell ill and it was revealed only their seventh daughter could save them. The royal couple despaired, believing their daughter dead, but Pari undertook a most dangerous journey for them — traveling to the Dragon's Heavenly Kingdom of the Western Sky for a plant that grew there. She had many hardships there and was forced to marry the Dragon King, to whom she bore seven sons. At long last, he allowed her to return to the palace with the cure, but she was too late. She found her parents dead. Oh, that she had come sooner, she cried! But she tried the remedy, anyway, and lo! The king and queen returned to life, and rejoicing in the return of their daughter. A happy ending, Grandmother, for all her suffering.

But as the old *mudang* sang this story, she began to weep, for shaman priestesses believe they are like Princess Pari, whose name means "to be thrown away." They, too, travel deep into the spirit world and suffer many hardships to bring back wisdom to the living. They deal with the dead all day long, but there are no happy endings for them. They are often reviled and made outcasts for their strange behavior. Listening to the Pari story, I felt ashamed, Grandmother. For I, too, had looked down upon the old *mudang* and thought her unclean and beneath me. But she is a just a poor old woman, and her life has been very hard.

But even as the Pari story ended, the *mudang*'s voice changed again. She was calling on the god *Ch'ilsŏng,* her special patron, to descend and possess her. She began to spin dizzily, so fast I could hardly follow her with my sleepy, teary eyes. The beating of her drum grew more frantic and loud, until its very beat seemed to take up residence in my chest. Her assistants followed with their own instruments and the rhythm raised us to our feet. Mother's sister-in-law began to dance, leaping and calling out. Sŏnwha soon threw herself into the dance, and before long, Mother's waiting women and Ch'ŏn-myong, and even Mother, herself — quiet, self-contained Mother — began to spin with the music. I felt myself compelled to dance as well, Grandmother, as if some enchantment had been placed on me. I was outside my body, outside of my mind. I saw the *mudang* through a haze of incense and lantern smoke. She was wearing a silvery *chima* covered in stars and she began to speak in a low, masculine voice.

"Ma-ya, Queen of Chinp'yŏng. Your time is through. You have given Silla its ruler. None shall replace her. Take the water from your husband's well and leave all behind."

Mother fell to her knees sobbing, overcome by the voice of the god and the whole experience. All of her women fell sobbing beside her.

"No!" I cried, grabbing hold of the old *mudang* and shaking her. "You do not speak true!"

But even as I laid my hands upon her, the woman's eyes rolled back into her head until only the whites showed. I felt the chill of holding a cold, empty body. Her mouth opened and shut like a puppet and the voice that issued forth was manly and terrifying.

"You, Sŏndŏk, future queen of Silla. You belong to

me," said the voice. "I send you starry visions, but still you deny me. Without roots, how long until the tree comes crashing down?"

I fell back from the old woman like one who has embraced lightning. It seemed to me the woman disappeared and in her place stood the god from the altar, the stern man with the halo of stars. I felt myself lifted into his arms, then we were speeding into the night sky. I looked down upon the lights of my aunt and uncle's house, on the torches of Kumsŏng, on the lanterns glowing outside the doors of Half-moon Fortress. The air was so thin, I could hardly breathe, and just as I was losing consciousness, I felt myself placed inside the ladle portion of the Great Northern Dipper as inside a jeweled chest, and cast off into the heavens. Dimly, in my delirium, I remembered that the astronomers call the four stars that make up the ladle of the dipper the Celestial Prison, for it is believed criminals of the royal family are sent here after death.

With that, I fainted, Grandmother, and it was a long time until I woke up.

13th day of the 8th moon, 17th year of King Chinp'yŏng

I am still trying to make sense out of what occurred at the *kut*, Grandmother. There was nothing logical or scholarly or measured about what happened to me. It was dark and primal and as ancient as the stars themselves. Did the god *Ch'ilsŏng* really say I belonged to him, or was it just an elaborate hoax? I am confused and tired and sad. Mother now seems completely resigned to entering the monastery and I am at a loss. I feel paralyzed by my doubts, as if I were still locked inside the Celestial Prison of my vision.

14th day of the 8th moon, 17th year of King Chinp'yŏng

The Hangawi festival is tomorrow and we must prepare for the weaving contest. How am I supposed to go about the routine of my day when everything I have ever known to be true is called into question? Am I a daughter of the Buddha or of the shaman god *Ch'ilsŏng*? Do I reject the stars or embrace them? And what of Confucius and his ideal of subservient womanhood? I feel torn in too many directions. I do not know who I am.

15th day of the 8th moon,
17th year of King Chinp'yŏng
Ch'ubun (Autumn Equinox) Hangawi Festival

Mother came to me this morning to wish me well with the weaving contest. She does not want to go out among the people for fear of stirring up trouble. There are many people who love my mother, and many clansmen who would gladly fight on her behalf.

I was so full of melancholy when she came in, I could barely rise to greet her, Grandmother. She climbed onto my pallet and pulled me into her lap, like she did when I was a little child. She kissed my head many times and wished me good fortune today.

"Mother, I do not want to go out among the people," I said. "I cannot pretend all is well when my heart is breaking. How can I possibly weave?"

"Dearest daughter," Mother whispered into my hair, "you spend so much time trying to please everyone that I sometimes fear you forget who you truly are. I have always loved you for your strength and bravery. Trust yourself this day. Let what is inside you come out. Your heart will know what to weave."

Later

Mother's words guided my hand today during the weaving contest, Grandmother. I do not know what has happened, but I know I have been changed by it.

While others wrestled or played on swings or watched puppet shows, my sisters and I led our teams of waiting women before a huge crowd of peasants. These workers knew nothing of the internal struggle I had been suffering, I realized. They were looking to me to set an example for their daughters, and I could not disappoint them. I pushed all my dark thoughts away and remembered Mother's words this morning. I let myself surrender to the loom. The weaving lasted all morning and late into the day. When, at last, the sun set and we stepped back from our work, the results were remarkable.

Ch'ŏn-myong's team had created a tapestry woven in lovely pearl-gray hemp with purple and yellow. Their scene showed a baby carried upon its mother's back in the fashion of peasant workers in the rice paddies. It was a fruitful fabric, bursting with foods of the harvest and happy children. It exactly expressed my second sister's character.

Sŏnwha's tapestry reflected her personality as well. Her team wove in bolder reds and greens. Their fabric depicted a lovely young woman wading in a stream, walking toward the west, where the sun was setting. The small figure of a man peeked around the border, beckoning the young woman. It was a singular work and very beautiful.

I barely remember weaving my tapestry. The women on my team said that my fingers flew over the loom, barely lighting on the shuttle before I was adding more strands of color. They swore the Weaving Maid had entered my body and done the work for me. When the tapestry was done, I wiped my eyes and saw I had woven what looked to be a compass. To the east, I had woven a deep pink peony flower in full bloom. To the south, I had woven a book, complete with Chinese characters. To the west, I had woven a pagoda, like the one I saw in my vision of Chajang and me at Hwangyŏng Monastery, and to the north, I had woven the seven stars of the Great Northern Dipper. In the middle of the tapestry rose a structure I had seen nowhere but in my dreams. A soaring tower that I thought of as *Ch'omsŏngdae* — my stargazing platform. Its base was square like the earth, and its round tower rose to meet the Dipper.

The peasants were delighted with my weaving, and I was voted the winner of the contest. But I believe I won a deeper victory today, Grandmother. Staring at the tapestry that I had unconsciously woven, I realized I have all these things within me: royalty, and scholarship, and religion, and astronomy, and even weaving — women's work I once hated. This newfound knowledge feels like a weak, green rice shoot, easily trampled or destroyed. Grandmother, please make me a good farmer. Please grant me the ability to nurture this new inkling of self.

20th day of the 8th moon, 17th year of King Chinp'yŏng

Mother leaves today. As a young bride, she brought water from her own father's well, so that it might intermingle with that of her husband's. Now she stands at the well at Half-moon Fortress, drawing a bucket to take to the home of the Buddha. We girls are all crying, and even Father weeps. He has not ceased to love Mother, but he believes his duty as king is to provide his country a male heir. The girl Seung-man stands modestly with her parents. She looks more petrified than triumphant, Grandmother. If it is the will of Heaven that she bear my father a son, so be it. In the meantime, I will work to accept myself.

Earlier this morning, I shaved my mother's lovely head. Her hair had barely a strand of gray and fell in waves to the ground. She always wore it in a thick knot at the nape of her neck, but for a moment — before it was sacrificed — it flowed around her body like something restless and alive. I cut it close to her skull with the scissors, then carefully shaved it smooth with an obsidian razor. She thanked me for my gentleness. I am surprised I did not cut her, Grandmother. I could barely see through my tears.

We will be allowed to visit Mother at her monastery on Nam-san mountain, where I once took comfort in the nun's chants against the tigers. But though we may visit, it will not be the same. She will not be here to comfort us or to lead by her wise example. I think of all the times I fought with her or took her for granted, and I make a vow to appreciate everyone and everything around me. We never know when all might be lost.

Good-bye, Mother. Sing to keep the tigers away.

1st day of the 9th moon,
17th year of King Chinp'yŏng
Hallo (Cold Dews)

It is the beginning of cool weather, when we say that the sky is high and horses are fat. I checked Moonbeam and she seems as slender and lively as ever. The sky does seem especially far away, though. There is no mist over the mountains, and they stand stark and sharp against the azure dome of the heavens. Mother is tucked away on one mountain, and Chajang on another. I exist in this valley, hemmed in by streams and stone and ancestral grave mounds.

9th day of the 9th moon, 17th year of King Chinp'yŏng

Father and Seung-man were wed today. I carried one of the pair of wooden duck standards, symbolizing marital fidelity and eternal union. The standards had been carried for Mother years before. For all the good they did her.

11th day of the 9th moon, 17th year of King Chinp'yŏng

Father's new wife has asked that I sleep with her in her chambers on nights when Father does not keep her company. She is not comfortable in the dark and can only fall asleep when there is a night lantern lit, and she is surrounded by waiting women. I still think of them as my mother's rooms, and it makes me sad to be there.

Still, I find it difficult to be angry at Seung-man, Grandmother. She is so pretty and wants so badly to be liked. She has large, soft eyes and such a slender waist I feel I could snap her in half. She did not choose to be queen, but is merely a pawn of her family's ambition.

Today I took her to the kitchens where she was to supervise the making our household's *kimchi*. All across the kingdom, salt is being rubbed into vegetables and barrels are being buried thus to last the winter. The year's pickling has begun.

Mother used to love to supervise the making of our winter *kimchi*. She brought special recipes from her parents' home, and even plunged her hands deep into the brine to lovingly work in the salt. The new queen has never had authority over a household and so stood in the kitchen helplessly, watching the cooks go about their business, without being able to offer guidance. Our old cook (she who always fed me forbidden sweets) made bold to ask the new queen if she had a *kimchi* recipe of her own. "No, use the old queen's," poor Seung-man replied, with her eyes cast down. "I always liked her *kimchi* best."

13th day of the 9th moon, 17th year of King Chinp'yŏng

As a gesture of friendship, Seung-man hung the tapestries my sisters and I wove on Hangawi in her chamber. I fall asleep under them every night.

Outside our window, the orange persimmons hang upon the trees like glowing harvest moons, and the smell of drying sesame fills the air. This season is dearest of all to the heart of a citizen of Silla. Yet for me, Grandmother, it is so melancholy.

15th day of the 9th moon, 17th year of King Chinp'yŏng Sanggang (Descent of Hoarfrost)

Everyone talks of the eclipse that is coming in fifteen days. The only thought that gives me comfort these days is knowing Lord Lin Fang will soon be proven wrong. Grandmother, I spent months doubting myself because of that man, but now I know better. He tried to kill my friend and he succeeded in banishing my mother. Lin Fang is what the philosopher Confucius calls "a small man." He embodies only the intolerant teachings of the Master, none of the wisdom.

20th day of the 9th moon, 17th year of King Chinp'yŏng

The day of Lin Fang's eclipse is close upon us, and preparations have begun in earnest for a Calamities-solving ritual. I have spoken my mind and there is nothing more I can do. If Father chooses to listen only to Lord Lin Fang, I can do nothing to protect him from himself.

21st day of the 9th moon, 17th year of King Chinp'yŏng

Lord Lin Fang is so puffed up with pride that he even invited me to play a game of chess today. He feels I am no longer a threat, now that Father has a new wife and, with luck, soon a new son. He can afford to be magnanimous.

It was a highly contested game. I quickly took his horse, and he took my chariot. We traded soldiers back and forth, and all was evenly matched. Then Lin Fang left himself open, and I had my elephant cross the river.

"What are you doing?" asked Lin Fang in annoyance. "That piece must stay on your side of the board."

"In our country's version of chess, the pieces are not so confined as they are in China's," I answered.

"I assumed we were playing by the Chinese rules," he responded tartly.

"You assume a great deal, my lord," said I.

After that, the play was aggressive, but the best Lin Fang could do was check my king with his king. This maneuver is a confession of a player's inferiority, because it is an admission that he or she cannot win the game.

"Lord Lin Fang," I exclaimed. "You have forced a draw."

"There is nothing else I could do," growled he. "If we were playing by Chinese rules, I would have taken your king."

"But you forget, sir," said I, "we are still in Silla, and we play by our own rules here."

I smiled politely and excused myself, leaving him fuming at the chess table.

A draw with Lin Fang suits me fine.

27th day of the 9th moon,
17th year of King Chinp'yŏng

A platform is being raised in the main courtyard of the palace and word has gone out far and wide announcing the Calamities-solving ritual. Originally, the platform was not properly oriented to the sun and Father was furious. He is very short-tempered with everyone these days. Mother would have known how to soothe him, but Seung-man is too timid.

28th day of the 9th moon,
17th year of King Chinp'yŏng

Legends say that a Fire Dog perpetually chases the sun, trying to devour it. On the rare occasions of an eclipse, the Fire Dog has managed to catch up and swallow a part or all of our sun. Soon enough, the sun burns his stomach and the Fire Dog must spit it out. Thus, the eclipse ends.

But those of us who understand science know that eclipses, like everything else, come in cycles. A formula says that we will have a total solar eclipse every eighteen years, eleven and one-third months, Grandmother. But knowing the science does not make the event any less terrifying. The king must perform a Calamities-solving ritual to end the eclipse. If he does not, there is always a chance the Fire Dog will not spit forth the sun, and the world will come to an end. As the protector of his people, a king may take nothing for granted.

1st day of the 10th moon, 17th year of King Chinp'yŏ Iptŏng (Winter Begins)

Today is the day of the eclipse, according to Lin Fang's Chinese calendar, Grandmother. According to my calculations, it is merely a day like any other.

I am too young to have ever experienced an eclipse, but I know the precautions that must be taken. You may not look directly at the phenomenon or the light from the sun will burn your eyes and strike you blind. Our astronomers have prepared a deep basin of water, blackened with Chinese ink. It will serve to reflect an exact image of the eclipse. The other safe way of observing the eclipse is to view it through a lens of semitransparent jade. My father had a jade looking glass prepared for that very purpose.

Lin Fang's calendar predicts the fateful event will oc-

cur early in the Horse hour, before the sun is directly overhead. We are to gather in the main courtyard of the palace
where a platform has been set up for the ceremony, and
where hundreds of drummers have been summoned to
raise a clamor and scare off the Fire Dog. I feel this is my
hour of truth, Grandmother. If the world goes dark today,
so do my illusions of ever becoming an astronomer.

Later, When All Is Done

I cannot remember ever having felt as tense as I did standing on the platform next to Father this morning. All of
our official astronomers had gathered. The entire courtyard was filled with lords and ladies of rank, as well
as common people who had crowded in to witness the
Calamities-solving ritual. An absolute silence seized the
courtyard, which seemed unnatural in a crowd so large. I
looked out onto a sea of pale, nervous faces; women on the
verge of fainting; men chewing their lips raw. Beside me,
my little cousin, Chindŏk, whimpered softly. I squeezed
her hand and told her all would be well.

When the time Lin Fang predicted approached, Father signaled the drummers to ply their mallets. Such a
cacophony of sound arose — brass bells, shrill pipes, the

deep-throated striking of gongs. In fear, the huge assembly of men and women began to keen and wail, adding their voices to the riot. Father laid himself flat on the platform, his arms in front of him, in the manner of the lowliest supplicant. Behind him, monks chanted prayers to Heaven, begging the sun not to depart, but to cast its healing rays upon the fields of Silla. The tension was almost too great to bear, and I considered for a moment throwing myself on the ground beside Father and begging Heaven's forgiveness.

But even as the clamor swelled, even as a groan tore at my own throat, I looked up at the sky and saw . . .

Nothing.

A brilliant blue, cloudless day to mark the beginning of winter. No shadow of the moon. No Fire Dog biting the heels of our blessed sun.

In their excitement, I believe the ritual participants barely noticed that the sky was still bright, that not a ray of sun had dimmed. But as long moments passed, Lin Fang began to look about worriedly. He shouted at the court astronomers to check their sundials and make sure that they had not misread the time. But all was correct. I noticed Father peeking up from his prone position, fixing a furious look upon Lin Fang. Seung-man, Sŏnwha, and

Ch'ŏn-myong crowded around me, half in awe and half in fear of Father's wrath should this eclipse not materialize. He would be humiliated, just as I feared.

Something had to be done, Grandmother. The drummers had become uncertain and the sky remained clear. If it were said Father did not know the will of Heaven, his reign would be forever compromised. I had to act.

I stepped forward and shouted for the drums to stop. A pall fell over the crowd, but I raised my voice triumphantly.

"People of Silla, you have witnessed a wonder today. Because of King Chinp'yŏng's powerful intervention, the Fire Dog has not dared to leave his den. The eclipse has been averted altogether. How powerful then is the king of Silla?"

A cry of approval went up among the common people, and I let out a huge sigh of relief. Lin Fang, however, looked ready to explode. His face was dark with fury, and I truly believe that if he had dared, he would have strangled me with his bare hands. But I had saved face for Father. I could not let him suffer humiliation at the hands of this arrogant man.

Father rose from the ground and accepted the adulation of his people. He bowed deeply, yet I saw his eyes were fixed on mine with a new respect, and I dared to believe, gratitude. I was once more his clever daughter Sŏndŏk. The spell of Lin Fang had been broken.

I woke last night in the new queen's chamber and found her night-light lantern softly illuminating the tapestry I had woven for the Hangawi festival. The peony and the book, the Buddhist pagoda, and the Dipper. And my stargazing tower in the center. *Ch'omsŏngdae*, as I think of it.

The new queen breathed softly beside me and the chamber was silent. All week, people had been whispering that I could foretell the future because I correctly predicted that there would be no eclipse. They did not stop to consider the hours I had spent calculating complicated figures to understand how the heavens work. They thought it was inspiration, nothing more.

And yet, when I look upon my tapestry, I almost wonder. How much of one's knowledge is hard work and how much is inspiration? I do not remember weaving these elements. Something deep inside me took over that day. If I can acknowledge my part in learning, should I not acknowledge that deeper mystery, too?

I lay there for some time, gazing at the woven *Ch'omsŏngdae,* as complete as if I had actually built it, brick by brick. As I watched its image flicker in the lantern light, I thought I heard a voice speaking low in my ear. The new queen was asleep. It could not have been her. And besides, the voice was deep and silvery masculine. It said, "Will you forsake me forever, Sŏndŏk? Will you refuse to water your roots?"

I let that voice seep into my chest, Grandmother, where I felt it vibrate for a very long time. I had heard it before — from the mouth of the old *mudang,* on the night of my mother's *kut.* But this time the voice seemed to encompass many different voices. It was the stern god *Ch'ilsŏng's* voice, and yet it had the slight intonation of Chinese Lin Fang. The bass notes sounded like Chajang, and the higher register reminded me of Mother's soft speech. It was the voice of my entire experience — good and bad — and it asked only one thing of me: to be acknowledged.

I rose from my pallet and carefully crawled over the new queen. Picking my way through the sleeping waiting women, I let myself out of the hall and waded through the night's fingery mist to the spot where I had once made my calculations, where I had intended to build *Ch'omsŏngdae*.

I made a promise to you, Grandmother, that I would give up stargazing if you spared the life of my friend Chajang. But Lin Fang's defeat has made me realize how much I miss the heavens. I believe I was wrong to make that promise, Grandmother, for in doing so I swore away a vital part of myself.

With trembling hands, I dug up that lacquered box of instruments I had buried. It was still there, like an acorn a squirrel might hoard against winter famine. Inside, my golden armillary sphere, my charts, abacus. My girlish writing before Lin Fang taught me proper Chinese calligraphy, and my elegant hand afterward. A starry history of this past year, and a piece of myself.

The crescent moon was but a thumbnail in the sky. I held my armillary to my eye and adjusted it against the horizon. Numbers and angles came flooding back and I could not write them down quickly enough. But I felt myself calculating in a new way last night, Grandmother. I was measuring, yes, but I was also trying to feel the stars rise and set inside my body. I was trying to become one with the heavens, instead of a mere observer.

I began to water my roots.

15th day of the 11th moon,
17th year of King Chinp'yŏng
Tŏngji (Winter Solstice)

More than a month passed since last I wrote to you, Grandmother. Forgive me. There has been much to do, and much to teach Seung-man.

It is once more the shortest day of the year, and a great deal has happened since I first took over our Ancestor Jar. I lost Chajang, and I lost Mother. I tried to be many things to many people, and in so doing almost lost myself.

In the philosophy of *um–yang*, Grandmother, we say that when night reaches its peak, daylight begins. It is the same with the changing of the seasons, and the mystical Chinese calendar flower. The moon waxes toward full and then begins to wane. We reach the dark new moon, and light is reborn.

Things could not have gotten any darker than the *mudang*'s *kut* and the loss of Mother. But Seung-man is not a cruel and hateful stepmother, and I believe we can be like sisters, even though I must call her Queen.

Lord Lin Fang is greatly subdued since the Eclipse That Never Happened. I will not gloat, though I cannot help but be proud of our native abilities, and our special relationship to the heavens. Like a waning moon, his power over Father has weakened, yet I will be almost sorry to see Lin Fang fall dark. Though his methods of instruction were not to my liking, he opened my eyes to a great many things. Unbeknownst to him, through observing his behavior as well as attending his lessons, I gained invaluable insight into the mind of our most powerful neighbor. As Father once said, "An ignorant queen is a conquered queen." Should fate ever choose me for the throne, I shall approach China with my eyes open.

But most of all, Grandmother, I feel this year has brought me closer to the *um–yang* within myself. I am a child of the Buddha. But I am also a child of the *mudang* and the shaman god *Ch'ilsŏng*. The old ways are feminine and they are *um*. The new ways are masculine and they are *yang*. I know if I can hold both in my heart, I will live the *um–yang* balance that is the harmony of the universe. Dark and Light. Male and Female. Knowledge and Intuition.

When the winter solstice returns, the earth will soon awake. When night reaches its darkest, daylight begins. A good queen should always remember this.

Perhaps Father's new wife will bear him a son, and I will never have a chance to govern well. But judging from the sky today, the heavens seem to think differently. The entire court has come outside and stands staring upward.

Their jaws drop and they cast awed glances at me. Even Lord Lin Fang looks at the sky and trembles.

The planet *Kumsŏng* is shining in the daytime, Grandmother. What is normally only seen at night is perfectly visible in the brightest day. And as you know, legend has it that when *Kumsŏng* shines by day, a woman is to rule. And there *Kumsŏng* shines. And here I stand.

Can we put our faith in the stars, Grandmother? Do they always speak true?

I believe they do.

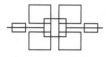

Epilogue

Sŏndŏk received the ultimate answer to her question in the year 632 (Western Common Era), when her father, King Chinp'yŏng, died without having produced a son. Sŏndŏk assumed the throne as the first woman ever to rule in eastern Asia in her own right.

Deep in the mountains of China, where he had gone to study the ways of the Buddha, the monk Chajang was having a dream. A Bodhisattva appeared to him saying, "Your kingdom is now ruled by a frail woman, and other countries will take advantage. You must return home and build a nine-story pagoda to honor the Dragon Spirit of Hwangyŏng Monastery who is now protecting Silla. The nine stories will represent your nine neighbors, and soon they will surrender and send tribute to the city Kumsŏng."

Chajang hurried back to Silla, where he and Queen Sŏndŏk were reunited. Together they undertook to build what would become the famous nine-story wooden pagoda at Hwangyŏng, which in its day stood a staggering 244 feet tall. The reunion of Chajang and Sŏndŏk marked the flowering of Buddhism in Silla. Together, they built many famous temples and monasteries. Chajang even brought back a bone of the True Buddha, which was interred at the foot of the nine-story pagoda.

But Sŏndŏk did not forget her love of the stars. In the second year of her reign she undertook to build her *Ch'omsŏngdae* (Nearer the Stars Place), or stargazing platform. It still stands today, the oldest astronomical observatory in the Far East, and the pride of modern Korea. The number of stones used to build it was 365, exactly the number of days in the year. There are twelve rectangular base stones to represent the months and figures of the zodiac, twelve stones from the base to the windowsills, and twelve above. Its total height is constructed of twenty-seven tiers of stone, and Queen Sŏndŏk was the twenty-seventh ruler of Silla. It is almost certain that a wooden platform made the tower even higher, but modern scientists are not absolutely sure as to how the tower was used. It is shrouded in mystery.

Queen Sŏndŏk dazzled her subjects with her ability to prophesy, much as had the ancient shaman priestesses. She made three famous predictions, according to the *Samguk Yusa (Memorabilia of the Three Kingdoms)*. The first is the story of the peonies having no smell, which is related in this diary. The second involved an invasion by a Paekche Kingdom army. Sŏndŏk heard a hoard of white frogs croaking by Jade Gate pond during the winter. The croaking frogs she took to mean angry soldiers. Their whiteness meant they were coming from the west (a direction symbolized in astronomy by the color white); and Jade Gate was a term related to women. She thus sent her generals to Woman Valley in the western part of Silla where they captured two thousand Paekche soldiers who had just crossed the border. Sŏndŏk's final prophecy correctly identified the hour of her own death.

Sadly, Sŏndŏk's reign was marred with constant fighting. Her enemies did take advantage of her being a woman and constantly threatened her borders. Nor was Queen Sŏndŏk safe at home. A faction of True Bone Silla nobles attempted to overthrow her but were defeated by her loyal general, Kim Yu-shin. Operating under the theory that "the enemy of my enemy is my friend," Sŏndŏk made alliances with the new T'ang Dynasty in China, which had been attempting to take Koguryŏ for years. She was forced to tread lightly, and maintain a perfect balance to keep from being swallowed by the powerful T'ang. She saved Silla from ruin by her pro-China policy.

Though Sŏndŏk had taken a consort king, she herself

failed to produce a male heir. When she closed her eyes for the final time in the year 647, she passed the throne to her female cousin, Chindŏk, the last of the Holy Bone. Chindŏk continued Sŏndŏk's alliance with China and the wars with Koguryŏ and Paekche. When she herself died childless in the year 654, the crown passed to Sŏndŏk's nephew, Mu-yŏl, her younger sister Ch'ŏn-myong's son. He was the first True Bone king of Silla and the restrictive bone rank system died with him. Under Mu-yŏl, the golden age of Silla began. He used the T'ang to conquer Koguryŏ and Paekche, then fought off the T'ang. The Korean peninsula was subsequently known as Unified Silla, and became a center for great art, poetry, and Buddhist philosophy.

Sŏnwha, Sŏndŏk's youngest sister, gave birth to a king as well, but it is told that this came about in a far more unusual and romantic way. Mattung, a clever young man of Paekche, saw the princess one day and was instantly smitten by her beauty. He vowed to steal her and taught the children of Kumsŏng a scandalous song to sing:

"Princess Sŏnwha
Hoping for a secret marriage
Went away at night,
With Mattung in her arms."

The allegation that Sŏnwha had lost her virtue so upset King Chinp'yŏng that he exiled the innocent young princess, sending her off alone with only the clothes on her back and a bag of gold. She wandered for several days in the mountains before she met a helpful young man, who offered to escort her. He turned out to be Mattung, and as her trust in him grew, she fell in love and eventually married him, fulfilling the words of the song. The people of Paekche so loved clever Mattung that they eventually raised him to be king, and he ruled with his queen, Sŏnwha, under the name King Mu.

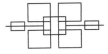

Historical Note

History of Ancient Korea during the Three Kingdoms Period

At the time Queen Sŏndŏk ruled, Korea was divided into three separate kingdoms: Konguryŏ to the north, Paekche to the southwest, and Silla to the southeast. Because of its harsher climate and its proximity to the conquering China, Koguryŏ was considered the most warlike of the three. Paekche lay farther away from Chinese aggression and was strongly influenced by Buddhism. Silla, even more remote from the mainland, was recognized as the most artistic and cultured of the Three Kingdoms. Buddhism reached Silla much later than its neighbors, and so native forms of religion, such as Shamanism, had much stronger roots.

These three kingdoms coexisted uneasily, and over the centuries, each tried to conquer the others. There was incessant warfare throughout the reigns of Chinp'yŏng, Sŏndŏk, and Chindŏk, and the strife only came to an end in the year 668, when Silla, in allegiance with the T'ang dynasty of China, conquered the entire peninsula. China assumed that Silla would become a dependent state, but they were surprised when Silla resisted and maintained its autonomy. Unified Silla, as the three kingdoms became known, promoted Buddhism and the arts, and a period of peace and prosperity followed.

By the mid-eighth century, Unified Silla was in decline. Members of the lower "head-rank" class waged a revolt against the True Bone rulers, and restored Paekche and the new Later Koguryŏ. One last queen ruled during this time of strife — Queen Chinsŏng (887–97), but she was acknowledged as a weak and corrupt queen, and had none of the statecraft that allowed Sŏndŏk and her cousin to rule successfully. Silla came to an end after 993 years of existence, when the last king, Kyŏng-sun, abdicated in favor of King Wang-gŏn, who established the Koryŏ Dynasty (918–1392). It is from Koryŏ that we get the modern name Korea.

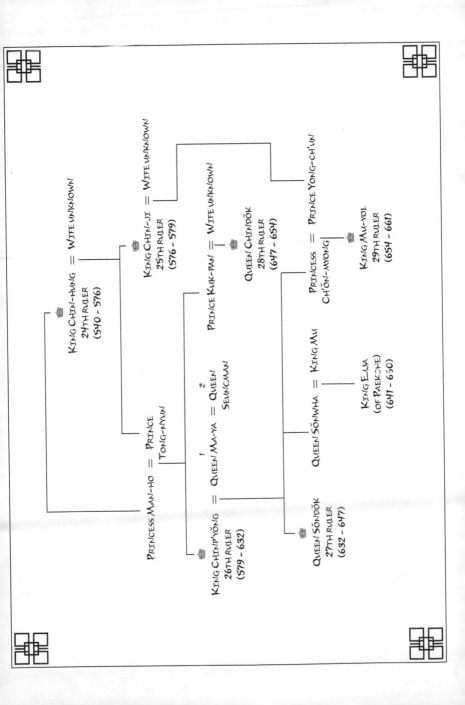

Sŏndŏk's Family Tree

In Silla, it was not written in stone that the eldest son would always inherit the throne. Sometimes a younger brother or nephew did, if he was deemed a wiser or better ruler. In Sŏndŏk's case, there were no male heirs living, and thus she became the first queen to rule Silla in her own right. The family tree chart shows what is known of Sŏndŏk's lineage, beginning with her great-grandfather. Dates of births and deaths (when available) are noted. The crown symbols indicate those who ruled. Double lines represent marriages; single lines indicate parentage.

King Chin-hung: 24th ruler (reigned 540 - 576) Sŏndŏk's great-grandfather. He came to the throne at age seven, with his mother as regent. During Chin-hung's reign, the *hwarang* were established, the *kayagum* was imported, and Hwangyong Monastery was built.

King Chin-ji: 25th ruler (reigned 576 - 579) Sŏndŏk's great-uncle. Sŏndŏk's grandfather, Tong-nyun, was King Chin-hung's eldest son but he did not rule; his younger brother Chin-ji ruled instead. Chin-ji died young, and his son was passed over in favor of Sŏndŏk's father, Chinp'yŏng. Later Chin-ji's grandson would become King Mu-yol, who began the unification of Silla.

King Chin-p'yŏng: 26th ruler (reigned 579 - 632) Sŏndŏk's father. He was the son of Prince Tong-nyun and Princess Man-ho (who was also Chin-hung's younger sister). Chinp'yŏng reigned longer than any other king of the Kim clan, a full fifty-three years.

His younger brother, Kuk-pan, was Queen Chindŏk's father. Chinp'yŏng married twice but had no male heirs; and thus Sŏndŏk, his eldest daughter from his first marriage, inherited the throne.

QUEEN SŎNDŎK: 27TH RULER (REIGNED 632 - 647) The first queen regent of any Korean kingdom. During her reign, she and the monk Chajang built the famous nine-story pagoda at Hwangyong Monastery, and Buddhism flourished. Most importantly, she constructed Ch'omsongdae, the oldest observatory in the Far East, which is still standing today. She died without an heir and passed the throne to her female cousin, Chindŏk.

QUEEN CHINDŎK: 28TH RULER (REIGNED 647 - 654) The second queen regent of Silla. She was the last of the Holy Bone rank to rule. Silla was at constant war during her reign, but the alliance Sŏndŏk had nurtured with China saved the kingdom from ruin.

KING MU-YOL: 29TH RULER (REIGNED 654 - 661) Grandson of King Chin-ji, son of Princess Ch'ŏn-myong, and Sŏndŏk's nephew. He was the first True Bone king to rule. During his reign, Silla conquered Paekche and the unification of the Three Kingdoms began. By the time his son, King Mun-mu, died, the Korean peninsula had become known as Unified Silla.

OTHER MEMBERS OF THE ROYAL FAMILY

QUEEN MA-YA: Chinp'yŏng's first wife and Sŏndŏk's mother. She gave birth to three daughters: Sŏndŏk, Ch'ŏn-myong, and Sŏnwha, but no son.

QUEEN SEUNGMAN: Second wife to King Chinp'yŏng. She also failed to provide an heir.

PRINCESS CH'ŎN-MYONG: Sŏndŏk's sister; Chinp'yŏng and Ma-ya's second daughter. She later married her cousin, Yong-ch'un, the son of King Chin-ji (25th ruler), and their son, Mu-yol, became the 29th ruler of Silla.

PRINCESS SŎNWHA: Sŏndŏk's sister; Chinp'yŏng and Ma-ya's third daughter. Legend tells that she was banished by her father when Prince Mu of Paekche fell in love with her.

Images of the ancient Queen Sŏndŏk are nonexistent. However, the face of this meditative figure, a bodhisattva known as Maitreya and one of the most revered Buddhist images, is said to have been modeled after Sŏndŏk. A bodhisattva, or "enlightened being," is a disciple of Buddha, a god or goddess who helps mankind.

A traditional Silla crown from the fifth and sixth centuries. Representative of the crown that Sŏndŏk likely wore, it is made of gold with numerous golden spangles attached to circular pieces of jade. The design has three stylized trees representing the cosmic world tree and two antler–like shapes evocative of the deer, a sacred animal in ancient Korea. Hence, it is sometimes called "the reindeer crown."

The Ch'omsŏngdae Observatory in Kyongju, South Korea. One of Sŏndŏk's most enduring achievements, this stargazing platform is twenty-eight feet high and composed of 365 stones (one for each day of the year). Ch'omsŏngdae is the oldest remaining astronomical tower in the world.

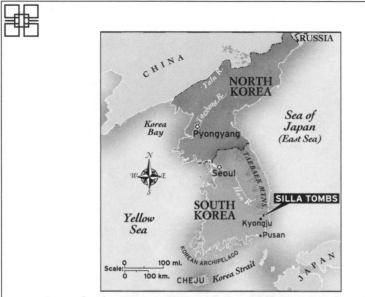

A map of modern Korea. South Korea's major city, Kyongju, is the former Kumsong.

Built in A.D. 528 and expanded in later centuries, Pulguksa is one of the oldest and most well-known Buddhist temples in Korea. Located just outside of Kyongju, on the western slope of Mount T'ohamsan, this temple — with its sweeping hipped roof and graceful staircase bridges — is an example of the great architectural masterpieces of the Silla period.

174

From Buddhism's early beginnings in Korea, images of the Buddha have been common-place. This eleven-foot-tall, solid granite Buddha is found in the Sokkuram cave-grotto shrine at Pulguksa Temple. It dates back to the Unified Silla Dynasty, A.D. 750, and many people feel that this very solemn, serene figure is the ideal representation of Buddha.

A portrait of Master Kung Fu-zu, Confucius. This undated illustration of the philosopher is based on a stone carving found in the forest of the Stelae in China.

A stone ice house in Kyongju. Though from a period much later than the Silla Dynasty, this is a common style of stone ice house from that time. Here blocks of ice were stored, and for some people, this was a cool, solitary retreat for religious meditation.

A modern–day shaman priestess during an initiation ritual. The history of shamanism in Korea dates back to its most ancient times. Shamans, also known as mudang, *serve as conduits for the gods and discontented ancestral spirits. Although once heavily consulted, today they no longer have such a prominent role in Korean society.*

The um *and* yang *symbols, also known as the yin–yang universal forces. The* um *is feminine, the negative force, while the* yang *is the positive masculine force. The two forces must remain in balance for a harmonious existence.*

The mounded tomb of Queen Sŏndŏk, who died in A.D. 647. During the Silla Dynasty, fifty-six mounded tombs were created for the various kings and queens of the period. Through limited excavations, it has been discovered that the tombs often contain numerous possessions of the deceased.

About Confucianism, Buddhism, and Shamanism

While the official state religion of both Silla and China was Buddhism, Confucianism played an extremely important role in daily life. Confucianism is not a religion, but a social and political philosophy based on the teachings of Master Kung Fu-zu (or Confucius). This philosophy is very complex, but in its simplest form it encourages good conduct and respect for proper social order. Filial piety (respect for one's parents and ancestors) is extremely important. Confucianism was far more rigid in China than it was in Silla during the Three Kingdoms period. Later, during the Koryŏ and Chŏsŏn (1392–1910) dynasties, Confucianism took much stronger hold and resulted in strict segregation of the sexes. The period in which Sŏndŏk lived was a time of relative freedom for women. It would have been almost inconceivable for her to rule later.

Buddhism, the religion of Chajang and the royal court of Silla, originated in India. Buddhists believe that all life is suffering and that only through detachment can a human overcome suffering. The concept of *karma* was extremely helpful to the ruling class of Silla because it taught that everything a person had on Earth was a product of his or her behavior in a past life. Thus, the king must have been very good and enlightened to have been born the king and not a peasant. Sŏndŏk was first and foremost a Buddhist queen, and with the help of the monk Chajang, left behind some of the most impressive and ancient Buddhist temples in Korea.

Shamanism is a more ancient belief system than either Confucianism or Buddhism, and has been practiced on the Korean peninsula since prehistoric times. Korean shamanism has been traced to the tribes of Siberia, based on the similarity between the reindeer antler crowns of both peoples. Because shamanism is often practiced by women, it has the reputation of being superstitious and primitive. During the Koryŏ Dynasty, female shamans, or *mudang*, were marginalized, and during the Chŏsŏn Dynasty outlawed, but earlier they had played an important role in court life. The second king of Silla, Nam-hae, took a title meaning "sorcerer" and was acknowledged as king of the shamans. Sŏndŏk herself was known to prophesy and, thus, was considered a shaman queen. Shamanism is not a religion, nor a philosophy. It has no hierarchy or priests or students. A shaman "illness" usually descends upon a woman, causing her to fall into a trance and to fear that she is going insane. This may last for days or even years, until she gives in and recognizes her spirit god.

Then she often apprentices herself to an older, more experienced shaman to learn the songs and dances of her new role.

Unlike Christianity, neither Confucianism, Buddhism, nor Shamanism are mutually exclusive. A person might practice all three at different times of life — engaging in ancestor worship on New Year's Day, offering prayers at a Buddhist temple, and consulting a *mudang* over a health crisis. All three were swirling around Sŏndŏk's court and many believe she would have sought to unify them as best she could.

Glossary

Banchan: Traditional meals in Korea consist of many different small dishes called *banchan*. They would have been eaten then on individual small tables while sitting upon the floor.

Bone Rank: (kolp'um): Ancient inhabitants of Silla expressed kinship through bone rather than blood. Those at the highest strata of society were divided into two bone ranks: Holy Bone (songgol) and True Bone (chin'gol). Only those of the Holy Bone might inherit the throne. It is still unclear exactly how bone rank was passed down in a family, but many scholars suspect it passed through the mother's side. With the death of Chindŏk, the Holy Bone died out in Silla, and thenceforth only those of the True Bone ruled.

Changgo: Ritual drum of the *mudang*; it was shaped like a modern–day hourglass.

Chima: Long, pleated skirt.

Chogori: Long, wide–sleeved jacket that would have fallen above the knee for a person of low rank, and between the knee and ankle for a person of high rank. Belted just below the breast. Aristocratic men and women wore brightly dyed *chima* and *chogori*, but red was reserved for the royal family.

Ch'omsŏngdae: Stargazing platform erected by Sondok in the second year of her reign. It is the oldest surviving astronomical tower in the far east and a national treasure of Korea.

Hours of the Day: The traditional Korean day was broken down into twelve "hours," with each ruled by an animal of the zodiac. They correspond as follows:

11 pm – 1 am	Rat Hour
1 am – 3am	Ox Hour
3 am – 5 am	Tiger Hour
5 am – 7 am	Rabbit Hour
7 am – 9 am	Dragon Hour

9 am – 11am	Snake Hour
11am – 1pm	Horse Hour
1pm – 3 pm	Sheep Hour
3 pm – 5pm	Monkey Hour
5 pm – 7 pm	Fowl Hour
7 pm – 9 pm	Dog Hour
9 pm – 11 pm	Pig Hour

Hwabaek: Council of nobles comprised of members from the top clans in Silla. A king did not hold tyrannical power; he was required to consult with the *hwabaek* on important matters. The Silla *hwabaek* in 527 voted to officially adopt Buddhism. In 651, the *hwabaek* was abolished.

Hwarang ("Flower Princes" or "Flower of Nobles"): The *hwarang* are shrouded in mystery. They were an elite group of young men who studied poetry, music, and philosophy, and it is now assumed that their purpose was also military. Early sources suggest the first *hwarang* were young girls, but they lost the privilege because of internal jealousy!

Kayagum: Stringed musical instrument that has become a symbol of traditional Korea. It is believed to have been invented by the King of Kaya before his land was swallowed by Silla. The *kayagum* has twelve silken threads stretched over movable bridges and is played upon the lap.

Kimchi: Traditional pickled vegetables stored in large ceramic jars and buried underground in the winter. The spicy red pepper and cabbage *kimchi* of today would have been unknown to Sŏndŏk as red pepper is a New World food, but evidence of pickled, fermented vegetables dates to prehistoric times.

Kut: Lengthy, elaborate ritual, sometimes lasting for days, in which a *mudang* calls down the spirits. Involves sung stories, drum playing, and frenzied dancing.

Kwaha ("underfruit horse"): Very small type of pony originally imported from China, likely related to the *jorangmal* of Cheju Island, an equally small pony known for its endurance. It was called "underfruit" because it was so diminutive that it could pass easily beneath branches of fruit trees.

Kyono & Chingnyo: Two bright stars in the summer constellations that correspond to Vega and Altair in the West.

Mudang: Shaman priestess have been recorded in Korean history since its most ancient times, and the historical Sŏndŏk is written of as possessing shamanistic powers. Scholars believe that the tradition originated in Siberia and migrated south many thousands of years ago. The *mudang* acts as mediums for the gods and the unhappy spirits of ancestors, who instruct the living on how to behave. Many people in Korea still consult *mudang*. But the shamans have lost their position in society, and are often considered crazy, outcast old women.

Ondol floor: Traditional Korean heating system, whereby flues underneath the floor heat the living room. Historically, Koreans sat, ate, and slept on the floor of the primary living space. In Silla, the floor consisted of packed earth covered by varnished or oiled floor paper. The warmest spot, directly over the fire below, would be reserved for the guest of honor, or for the king.

Seasons: In Korea, the four greater seasons are divided into twenty-four "fortnight" seasons of two-week increments. The year begins in the spring with Ipch'un, and ends with Taehan. Along with many other Asian societies, Korea relies on the lunar calendar, which is based on phases of the moon, rather than the Western Solar calendar.

Ssirom: Traditional Korean wrestling match, associated with Tano Festival in which one man tries to pull another over by tugging on his belt. The prize was usually a bull.

Um & Yang: The yin-yang forces at work in the universe. The *um*, or *yin*, force represents all that is feminine, dark, adversarial, and cold; the *yang* force represents all that is male, active, positive, and bright. These forces must be kept in perpetual balance or a body becomes sick.

Yut: A New Year's stick game still played in Korea today that originated fortune-telling.

About the Author

Author Sheri Holman knew very little about the culture when she first thought of writing a book set in ancient Korea — she only knew she loved the food! What better excuse to go to Korean restaurants than to say she was doing "research?" As in most Far East Asian societies, women rarely ruled in their own right, and Ms. Holman became especially intrigued with the figure of Sŏndŏk, an astronomer queen known to prophesy. With more and more young women today excelling in mathematics and the sciences (as well as the arts), Sŏndŏk seemed like a wonderful role model and touchstone from the past.

" Sadly, almost nothing is known about Sŏndŏk's life — early or late. She was probably born with the name Dokman, but as she is best known by her queenly title, Sŏndŏk (which means 'sweet virtue'), I chose to have her called so throughout. Her three prophesies are all that were recorded of her beyond the dates she ruled and the buildings she erected. It is even uncertain exactly when she was born, though most scholars put it at A.D. 580. To recreate her life, I had to make many educated guesses. She was close in age to the famous monk Chajang, who would have been at court before King Chinp'yŏng threatened to have him put to death. Later, she and Chajang worked intimately to build many important Buddhist monuments. Sŏndŏk never had any children, and it is not so unlikely to believe she might have suffered the loss of one great love. As for her passionate interest in astronomy, I believe her later life made that clear. One of her first acts as queen was to erect Ch'omsŏngdae, an observatory unlike any ever raised before. She built this tower a full seven years before she helped Chajang with his nine-story pagoda. By this, I think we can guess where her heart truly lay.

"As for the other characters in the diary, Lord Lin Fang is completely fictitious, as is the old *mudang*. But everyone else in the diary really lived and breathed and walked the streets of Chumming, which is now modern-day Kyongju in South Korea."

This is Sheri Holman's first book for younger readers. She is the author of two highly-acclaimed, best selling adult novels, *A Stolen Tongue* and *The Dress Lodger*, which have been translated into over fourteen languages. She is currently at work on a third adult novel *The Mammoth Cheese*. She lives with her husband, Sean Redmond, their four cats, parrot, and brand-new daughter, Ella.

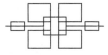

Acknowledgments

First and foremost, I'd sincerely like to thank Jungsoo Kim of New York University for her invaluable help unraveling the many obscurities of ancient Silla. I'd also like to thank my marvelous editor, Sonia Black and my friends at Scholastic, my beloved agent Molly Friedrich, Jean Marzollo, who took the trouble to teach me about the world of young adult literature, and of course Sean Redmond, my husband, friend, and now consummate babysitter . . .

Cover painting by Tim O'Brien

Page 171: Bodhisattva, Korean Cultural Service, New York, New York.

Page 172: Crown, Korean Cultural Service, New York, New York.

Page 173: Ch'omsŏngdae Observatory, SuperStock Images, Jacksonville, Florida.

Page 174 (top): Map of modern Korea, Jim McMahon.

Page 174 (bottom): Pulguksa temple, SuperStock Images, Jacksonville, Florida.

Page 175: Buddha, Korean Cultural Service, New York, New York.

Page 176 (top): Confucius, Bettmann/CORBIS, New York, New York.

Page 176 (bottom): Ice House, Korean Cultural Service, New York, New York.

Page 177: Shaman, Korean Cultural Service, New York, New York.

Page 178 (top): *Um* and *Yang*, Photodisk/Getty Images, New York, New York.

Page 178 (bottom): Sŏndŏk's tomb, Korean Cultural Service, New York, New York.

Other books in The Royal Diaries Series

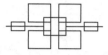

ELIZABETH I
Red Rose of the House of Tudor
by Kathryn Lasky

CLEOPATRA VII
Daughter of the Nile
Kristiana Gregory

ISABEL
Jewel of Castilla
by Carolyn Meyer

MARIE ANTOINETTE
Princess of Versailles
by Kathryn Lasky

ANASTASIA
The Last Grand Duchess
by Carolyn Meyer

NZINGHA
Warrior Queen of Matamba
by Patricia C. McKissack

KA'IULANI
The People's Princess
by Ellen Emerson White

To Ella, may this dedication be the first of many.

While The Royal Diaries are based on real royal figures and actual historical events, some situations and people in this book are fictional, created by the author.

Library of Congress Cataloging-in-Publication Data
Holman, Sheri.
Sŏndŏk, princess of the moon and stars / by Sheri Holman.
p. cm. — (The royal diaries)
Summary: In a series of messages placed in her grandmother's ancestral jar, a sixth-century princess and future ruler of the Korean kingdom of Silla vents her frustration at not being permitted to study astronomy because she is a girl.
ISBN 0-439-16586-5
1. Sŏndŏk, Queen of Silla, d. 647 — Juvenile fiction.   2. Silla (Kingdom) — Juvenile fiction.   3. Korea — History — To 935 — Juvenile fiction.
[1. Sŏndŏk, Queen of Silla, d. 647 — Fiction.   2. Silla (Kingdom) — Fiction.   3. Korea — History — To 935 — Fiction.   4. Princesses — Fiction.   5. Astronomy — Fiction.   6. Sex role — Fiction.   7. Diaries — Fiction.]
I. Title.   II. Series.
PZ7.H73265 So 2002
[Fic] — dc21   2001031146

12   11   10   9   8   7   6   5   4   3   2   1   02   03   04   05

The display type was set in Arnoval ITC.
The text type was set in Augereau.
Book design by Elizabeth B. Parisi

Printed in the U.S.A.
First printing, June 2002